A Mate of Their Own

Cauldron Falls, Volume 5

Solara Gordon

Published by THE EARTH MOVED, LLC, 2024.

A MATE OF THEIR OWN

First edition. August 4, 2024.

Copyright © 2024 Solara Gordon.

ISBN: 979-8988654971

Written by Solara Gordon.

Also by Solara Gordon

Cascade Bay
Love Reborn
Reunited By Choice
Love's Triple Play
Three Hearts In Love
For the Love of Three

Cauldron Falls
Believe In Love
Home for the Holidays
Three Hearts Entwined
A Mate of Their Own
A Christmas Reunion

Peyton Corners
Falling for You
Caught by Love's Slow Burn

Standalone
A Heart's Desire
To Love You Again

To Love You Again

Watch for more at https://solaragordon.com/.

This one is for my Readers, my Street Team, My Glamorous Stars! You inspire me!

Thank you to all my readers for their ongoing support and inspiration! Special Thank You to Chevy Allen for Beta Reading portions of the book.

Daniel, Kirk and Carla's story started out on a journey about three friends refinding themselves and the bond that brought them together in their youth. The story morphed into three people's second chance at love and finding a mate of their own.

I hope you enjoy Carla, Daniel and Kirk's journey rediscovering their love, their connection and the love that reunites them and bonds them together.

Smiles,

Solara Gordon

CHAPTER ONE

Carla Smith leaned back against the bar watching two male patrons close to the opposite end. One male's gaze met hers twice since he joined his companion an hour earlier. The guy with him gave her a hot once-over after he caught his buddy gazing at her.

The ginger-haired one drew her attention from her first glimpse of him. Redheads piqued her interest and hormones since high school and Kirk Addison's french kiss outback of the softball dugout their junior year. She swore Kirk's brown eyes glowed every time he looked at her. The guy with Red reminded her of Daniel McFarmer who tagged after Kirk and her until the three of them became fast tight friends. Daniel's close-cropped haircut never let on to his actual golden brown hair color. His hazel eyes glinted when she kissed him the time they'd played Spin-the-Bottle in her cousin's tree house.

Red caught her staring at him again. Carla fanned herself and looked away. Eye candy had its sweet moments. Keeping her mind focused on the customers at the bar and the servers' drink orders pushed perusing Red off her list of mental activities.

She shielded her eyes as she looked out over the congestion of tables and couples milling about at the edge of the dance floor. She smiled as a couple leaned toward each other, lips puckered. An old image flashed across her thoughts. Kirk and her in a similar stance their first kiss. Daniel had reciprocated on his turn. Playing Spin-the-Bottle with only the two of them had had its rewards.

Carla noted the two guys she'd been ogling making their way toward the tables at the back of the dining area. There was a familiarity to them. Part of her psyche kept pinging her like she knew them each time she looked at them. She shook her head. Her extrasensory perception had to be firing because of the high school reunion happening next weekend. Why were Daniel and Kirk on her mind tonight? Had the two guys at the bar ignited this trip down memory lane?

Daniel looked over his shoulder and turned back to Kirk. He grinned and nodded. "Carla keeps looking our way. She's interested."

"Good," Kirk responded. "Do you think she remembers us?"

"Maybe," Daniel began, glancing over his shoulder again. "Carla moved after our joint make-out session. We didn't get a chance to go further."

"Stop being obvious," Kirk retorted, elbowing him. "We lucked out when the matchmaking council approved our request."

Daniel saluted Kirk with his beer bottle and sat down at a table close to the kitchen. "We sure did. Here's to Cauldron Falls' newest triad—you, me, and Carla."

Kirk sat down and clinked his beer bottle against his. "And to Carla's agreement to being courted."

Daniel drank part of his beer and lowered the bottle, shaking his head. "I don't think there's a problem there. Don't forget Eva's report."

Kirk nodded, setting his bottle on the table. "Oh, yeah. Eva's report definitely swung the council in our direction."

Daniel shrugged as he placed his bottle on the table. "Eva said Carla admitted having two guys interested in her intrigued her."

"Could also be our stubborn holdout that we want to choose our mate." Kirk leaned toward him, lowering his voice. "Also doesn't look good when the nephews of the two eldest matchmakers in town are still single."

Daniel snorted. "Yeah, our aunts aren't going to let us off the hook until we've got a mate or they choose others for us."

Kirk grinned and asked. "What's our courtship plan?"

"We've got until the full moon to get Carla's agreement."

"Six weeks isn't a lot of time." Kirk pulled back, shaking his head. "Not gonna be easy."

"If we wanted easy, we'd gotten matched." Daniel raised his head and looked out over the crowd back at the bar to where he'd first seen Carla staring at him. "I like the chase to a point. Carla is what I want. You?"

Kirk set his bottle next to his. "Our partnership is solid. We know how each other works. I'm in."

Daniel nodded. "Okay. Operation courtship begins now."

Kirk held up his hand as he spoke. "Right. I saw Eva and our aunts making their way toward the back seating area."

Daniel high-fived Kirk. He watched Kirk turn away and walk toward where their aunts and Eva sat, waiting for their decision. A decision both he and Kirk had talked about many times. During their college years, the years each of them traveled building job experiences and the three failed relationships between them. Yes, Carla knew them then. Listened to their guy talk about the other girls. About the women who got their gonads hot and very bothered. She'd become their confidante, and they hers. Too bad her parents decided an all-witch community was better than Cauldron Falls mixed supernatural and magical one. That was about to change. The three of them had gotten another chance. A chance to build on their prior foundation and see if the relationship they'd all wanted before could happen this time.

Kirk combed his fingers through his curly hair. Gone were the crew cuts his ex-military father insisted upon. After he started letting it grow out, the riotous ginger-colored curls appeared grabbing his college nickname Curly. Women fawned over him as he came off the rugby field sweat-covered and his curls even more predominant. A few teased him about his tarnished lopsided halo to the point of calling him Angel. Neither nickname stuck for long thanks to his short-lived disastrous ROTC endeavors. His ankle still pinged when cold weather approached. A wolf with a limp stood out when the pack hunted. Hunting alone didn't work either. The game got away and well. . .feeding his animal half wasn't always successful. Praise deities, Daniel stood by him and helped when others shunned him. That was ceasing thanks to his and Daniel's new roles as dual pack alphas, a male witch and a shapeshifter. A new generation was in charge and they chose new ways of doing things. Now if their aunts would buy into their plan, maybe—just maybe mixed pair bondings would get the acceptance they deserved.

Kirk squinted as he moved deeper into the dimmer lighted area of the club. Music pulsed out of the overhead speakers around the dance floor. A single female moved toward him. He stepped right. She copied his move. Back and forth and side-to-side they maneuvered around the tight configuration of tables until he pulled a chair out from the table closest to him. "I'm not interested. I'm meeting someone." He pointed toward the table where the lavender lantern glowed center of the table. The signal his Aunt Zelda came up with announcing Cauldron Falls' matchmakers were in the house.

Daniel's Aunt Naomi's gaze caught his. She nodded and crooked her finger in a come-hither motion. Kirk swallowed hard. He didn't know who was more stubborn, Aunt Zelda or Aunt Naomi. Aunt Zelda won many a stare-down with her feline familiar. Tobias yowled, switched his tail and dove under the couch each time she won. Aunt Naomi out stubborned a local farmer's mule by sitting next to him for several hours and braying every time the pig-headed jackass did. In the end, both women garnered his and Daniel's respect. Their aunts lived life their way.

"About time you got here," Aunt Naomi yelled as the music stopped. Kirk inhaled and tapped his fingers twice against his jeans.

"Lower your voice, dear," Aunt Zelda said, laying her hand on Aunt Naomi's arm. "The music ceased."

"Thank you," Kirk offered, pulling out the chair at the head of the table. Eva, Carla's best friend, sat next to Aunt Naomi. He nodded as their gazes met. Eva dipped her head, not looking away. Sitting down, Kirk glanced at Aunt Zelda. She held a pack of Tarot cards in one hand.

"Do we let the cards decide or do you have something to tell us?" Aunt Zelda asked, fanning the cards face down across the table.

Aunt Naomi placed her hands on the table and leaned forward. The light from the lantern gave her an eerie almost ghostly three-dimensional appearance. Kirk blinked, looked down, and wiped his wet palms on his jeans.

"Daniel and I made our decision," Kirk said, placing his palms down on the table.

Aunt Martha nodded and leaned back. Aunt Zelda looked at Eva, who nodded and leaned toward the table. Aunt Zelda looked back at him and spoke. "What is your decision?"

Kirk swallowed, wet his lips, and replied. "We're courting Carla."

Eva snickered. "Don't you need her agreement to do so?"

"No," Kirk retorted. "We're courting her. She's the one we want."

"Well," Aunt Naomi began. Kirk leaned tighter to the table, holding up his hand.

"*We've decided,*" he repeated, this time with more emphasis. "You gave us until the next full moon to get Carla's agreement."

He gazed at each of the women, not blinking until he looked at the next. He leaned back, folding his arms across his chest. He sat upright, shoulders relaxed, looking at each of the women again. Too bad Daniel wasn't here to witness this. Kirk took a deep breath and relaxed against the back of the chair. "Uncle Zac retired. He named Daniel and I co-alphas. It's time our decisions and choices are honored as such."

Aunt Zelda glanced at Aunt Naomi who bobbed her head and looked down. Eva did the same and Aunt Zelda glanced back at him, copying Aunt Naomi's gestures. Kirk pressed his lips together, counting to five, and unfolded his arms. He scooted back from the table, rose and spoke. "Eva, when's Carla's next break?"

Eva glanced at her watch. "In five minutes. It's her meal break."

"Good. Get her to come over to the table close to the kitchen and sit with Daniel and me." Kirk started to turn away.

"She ain't a dog who comes just because you call her," Eva mocked, slapping her hands down on the table and standing.

Kirk curled his lips into his best thanks for your unsolicited comment smile and turned back to the table. "I get that. You're a great friend. Daniel and I want to talk with her. Nothing is going to happen without her consent and buy-in. Okay?"

Eva opened her mouth ready to probably deliver another snarky comeback. Eva's luck with arranged matches and marriages hadn't faired any better than his and Daniel's. Kirk didn't know if jealousy or envy fueled her remarks. Maybe it was best friends looking out for each other. He got that. To move through the fear, sometimes required walking with it.

Aunt Naomi spoke as she took ahold of Eva's wrist. "We're going to be right here. Remember, this isn't a done deal. If *Carla* says no, it's over. If *she* says yes, *they* move forward."

Kirk caught Eva's nod as she sat down. He walked away hoping that Eva got he and Daniel would honor Carla's decision. Neither of them wanted to hurt their intended mate.

Carla came out from behind the bar, her meal choice decided. The dinner special had her mouthwatering each time a server set the meal down in front of a patron. Roasted chicken falling off the bone, thick twice-whipped buttermilk mashed potatoes with pan-drippings gravy, corn and lima bean mix fresh from Chef Rory's greenhouse garden, and honey yeast rolls. As she moved toward the table close to the kitchen, she noticed the two guys she'd been gawking sitting at the table. Eva was talking with them. Three plates with the dinner special filled the table.

Eva looked up, waved and stood up. She walked toward her. She stopped a few feet from the table. Carla moved forward until she was almost toe-to-toe with Eva.

Eva glanced over her shoulder twice and licked her lips. Carla rolled her eyes. She knew that sign all too well. Eva's mothering instinct continuously smoldered, waiting for the spark to ignite it. Raising six siblings after her mother walked out on them and her globetrotting sister's twins left her on alert ready to spring into maternal mode at a moment's notice. Protecting those she cared about mattered most to Eva. Even her best friend.

Eva pointed back over her shoulder as she spoke. "Classmate reunions happening all over the place tonight."

"What are you talking about?" Carla leaned to her right, looking past Eva.

"Daniel and Kirk," Eva said, pointing over her shoulder again.

"Okay. And they're here for the reunion next weekend. So what?" Carla moved around Eva, glancing toward the table where Daniel and Kirk sat looking back at her.

"There's more to it." Eva sidestepped away from her. "Aunt Naomi and Aunt Zelda are here too."

"*I didn't ask or agree to a match.*" Carla shoved her empty hand into her pants pocket and wiped her palm on the interior fabric.

"They're here for those that did." Eva moved back in front of her, blocking her view of the table. "Take some deep breaths. Daniel and Kirk asked to talk with you. Go on, eat your dinner before it gets cold."

Carla nodded, stepping around Eva again. "And you?"

"Helping Aunt Naomi and Aunt Zelda out. Matchmaker apprentice on duty, you know." Eva smiled at her, winked and held up two fingers as she got even with her.

"Two fingers for what?"

"You don't have to agree to anything." Eva lowered one finger.

"Okay. What else?"

"Dinner with old friends and two hunks is pretty fine if you ask me." Eva grinned and lowered her second finger. "Besides, you've talked about having two guys interested in you at the same time."

CHAPTER TWO

Carla exhaled, shook her head and smiled. "I agree dinner and two hunks is *very fine*." She looked at Daniel and Kirk intently and back at Eva. "They look to have aged very nicely."

"So enjoy. You're safe. Your bouncers are close by. I don't think anyone is going to mess with the owner." Eva started to walk away.

Carla reached out, grabbing Eva's arm. Eva stopped and looked at her. Carla rubbed her lips together. She opened her mouth and immediately closed it. She dropped her hand and moved away from Eva. Daniel and Kirk had protected her in the past. She trusted them then. Surely, she could trust them now. Could she?

"You ready?" Daniel asked, watching Carla make her way toward them. She wore her hair shorter. She hadn't changed the color like many other women did as they aged. Her aura, like then, gave off a golden blondish glow much like her hair. Her breasts bounced much like they had with her determined walk in high school.

"As ready as I can be. You leading or me?" Kirk chuckled. "This food is getting to me."

Daniel replied, "Enjoy both views. You can enjoy the food in a moment."

"You're right," Kirk said. "Carla and a great meal. Not a bad way to start off the evening."

"I agree," Daniel said, standing up. He pulled out the chair opposite him and Kirk.

"Evening, Carla," Daniel said. He pointed at the chair. "Join a couple of old friends for dinner?"

Carla walked past the chair, stopped very close to him and rose on her tiptoes. "Sure. But this first."

Daniel blinked, pulled back a bit, and looked down. Carla, her lips puckered, came toward him. He glanced at Kirk who shrugged. Not quite the greeting either of them imagined, but why not. Cutting to the chase might move them steps ahead.

He leaned, tilting his head so his lips and Carla's would meet at an angle. The first time he kissed her, they'd spent the better part of five minutes cocking their heads, bumping into each other before they got their lips together.

Carla laid her hand on his arm and leaned closer. Her eyes closed. Daniel let go of the chair and slid an arm around Carla's waist. He wet his lips and closed the distance between them.

Soft, warm, and definitely very feminine lips met his. He felt Carla's short shuddered breaths and the short shiver that rippled through her. Heat grazed the palm of his hand where it lay close to the waist of her jeans. Similar warmth pooled where Carla's hand touched his arm. He brushed his lips over hers twice and started to pull away.

"No," Carla whispered and pressed tighter to him. Her hand slipped higher, reaching the crux of his elbow.

Daniel pulled Carla tighter to him, not wanting her to fall. He pressed his lips tight to hers and parted his lips slightly. The tip of her tongue met his. Moments passed as the tips dueled. Coughing sounded, pulling him out of the kiss. He pulled back, creating space between them, allowing air to wisp over their faces. He grinned as Carla's eyes opened. Daniel leaned close again, resting his forehead on hers. "Thanks, but we're in public."

Carla nodded, met his gaze and winked. She spoke as she rocked back on her heels. "Keeps the matchmakers wondering. You always did get me hot and bothered."

Kirk's laughter kept them from saying more. Daniel slipped his hand along Carla's waist until he touched the chair. He let go and moved away. He looked past her face. His gaze settled on the first thing Carla's five-five height allowed, her bust. He blinked, stared a few minutes more, enjoying the view and the more than handful bust gracing her curviness.

Carla stepped away from him and faced Kirk. "Good to see you too, Kirk."

She made her way around the table, glancing back the way she'd come. She stopped close to Kirk, leaned in and said, "Your turn."

Kirk nodded, raised his arm and laid his hand on Carla's shoulder. Daniel grinned as the two leaned closer. Their gazes unwavering like they were alone. Kirk puckered, tangling his fingers loosely in Carla's hair. Their lips met. Kirk reached up, cupping Carla's face. His thumb tracing her jawline as the kiss deepened. Daniel inhaled slowly, feeling the heat reach across the table and washing over him. His groin nudged his fly as their kiss lingered. He pressed his lips together and gripped the back of the chair. Compersion rocked through him. Watching Kirk and Carla enjoying their kiss sparked his joy. Enjoying their passion, heat and delight kindled his. He knew there wasn't competitiveness going on. Envy nipped at him. Not that Kirk and Carla were enjoying each other. Envy that couples somewhere behind closed doors were able to take their passion to the next level. Taking a deep breath, Daniel closed his eyes and exhaled. Time to take these kisses to the next level would happen when time and place allowed.

Daniel cleared his throat, ready to speak when the kitchen door swung open giving off a loud squeak. The noise jolted Kirk and Carla apart. She shook her head, glanced at him grinning, and rolled her shoulders. Kirk scooted away from Carla, grinning too.

Carla pulled the neck of her top away from her fanning herself as she moved back to the empty chair. "Steamy and scorching. That hasn't changed."

Daniel held the chair for her as she sat down. Consummate manners and a gentleman were the words she used to describe him when she confided her high school crush to Eva. Kirk had been rough around the edges then. Ready to rebel and grab the attention he felt missing from him. Two pierced ears and fake tattoos paired with ratty jeans and t-shirts with not quite raunchy slogans caused him to stand out and not always in a good way. How the pressed khakis and sport shirt dressed honors scholar and the punk rocker wanna-be nerd became fast friends few knew. She wondered how many would remember Kirk's transition their sophomore year after he'd won full scholarships to several major universities. Her and Daniel's tutoring paid off.

"Let's dig in," Carla murmured, looking at her plate. "Chef Rory's outdone himself tonight."

"Oh yeah," Kirk said, rubbing his hands together. "Never pass up good food."

Daniel and she burst out laughing. Kirk's appreciation for a well-cooked meal hadn't changed. He appeared as slim as she remembered him from the last reunion she'd attended five years ago. Daniel was already cutting into his chicken. He raised a fork full and spoke. "Here's to good eats!"

They passed the next fifteen minutes in comfortable silence as they ate. The loud squeaking kitchen door practically stopped as several of the servers sat at nearby tables consuming their evening meal. One in particular, wearing a nametag with Bertha on it, stopped next to their table. Carla looked up as Bertha spoke. "Boss lady, Chef Rory's threatening Frankie with his meat cleaver *again.*"

Carla laid her napkin on the table. "Thank you, Bertha. I'll take care of it." Carla pushed back from the table, glancing at Daniel and Kirk.

She spoke again as she stood. "Chef and his cat Frankie have a regular Saturday night melee about this time." She glanced at her watch. "Almost right on time. Something about eight PM and a female feline familiar that sets the two of them off."

Daniel clapped his hand over his mouth. He didn't cut off much of his laughter. Kirk's chortles sounded behind his napkin. Carla smiled and nodded. "Yes, one curmudgeon cat rules the roost with a talented four-star chef. He's one hell of a cook and a great mage. He calls it a curse. Others say it's a blessing."

Daniel lowered his hand. "Go take care of the cat from hell and her owner. We'll be here."

Daniel wiped his hands on his napkin and glanced at Kirk. He watched him, grinning like a Cheshire cat. Daniel shook his head, raised his water glass and drank. "I know about persnickety familiars. Sounds like Aunt Naomi's coven sister Zulia paired those two up."

Kirk laid his knife and fork down, and wiped his mouth. He picked up his water glass, saluted Daniel and replied. "I'm glad I don't have to worry about all this matching and pairing up beyond us mating with Carla. Too much angst, if you ask me."

"A lot of pairing up, for sure. Carla hasn't said yes yet." Daniel went back to eating.

"She hasn't said yes out loud. Those kisses weren't a no." Kirk drank from his glass and set it down. He picked up his fork. "Either way, not a bad start to the evening."

Kirk continued eating until only bones remained on his plate. Daniel's plate was the same. Carla's still sat where she'd left it over ten minutes ago. Kirk tossed his napkin on the table and started to scoot toward the end of his chair. "Maybe I need to get someone to check if she needs. . ."

The squeaking of the kitchen door swinging open cut him off. Carla, frowning and pushing up her shirtsleeves, entered the dining room. She nodded at Daniel and him. Sat down and sighed. "Frankie is a pain-in-the-ass possessive feline. She took a swipe at me. Seems the local roving romeo tomcat knocked her up and five kittens are making their bed in *Chef Rory's desk drawer*!"

Kirk pressed his teeth against his bottom lip. Snickering wasn't appropriate as much as he wanted to. Daniel glanced at him, back at Carla and shook his head. Of course, Daniel could zing him about the wild hunt six months prior. Wolf lust and a full moon didn't mix well. Looked like each of them had their share of lust-filled sexual passion results to deal with. Not that it was all bad. Sexy passion relieved angst pent-up frustrations and felt so good when the orgasms hit.

"You gonna be able to finish your meal?" Daniel asked, leaning back against his chair.

"Oh yeah. Stan, my relief bartender, clocked in while Chef Rory and I discussed Frankie's motherhood." Carla cut into the remaining chicken on her plate. She looked up, speaking again. "Talk to me about what's going on with you."

Kirk looked at Daniel, who nodded. Kirk rubbed his lips together, nodding back. He drank the rest of the water in his glass and spoke as he set it down. "I moved back to town a year ago. Settled on the outskirts near the new development Forest Park."

"Nice condos and single-family homes out that way. How about you?" Carla asked, pointing her fork at Daniel.

"Moved back about the same time. I closed on a house recently." Daniel leaned forward. "What about you?"

"Ten months ago." Carla shook her head and forked more chicken into her mouth. She chewed slowly. Talking about her past didn't set well with her. She'd learned the hard way about keeping her mouth shut. Damn her parents for not seeing beyond their prejudices. There were details she could let out and others she kept tightly guarded. She swallowed, drank water, and met Kirk's gaze. "Eva and I stayed in touch. She let me know Mr. Maxson wanted to sell the tavern."

Kirk nodded. "Never thought Mr. Maxson would retire."

Daniel snickered. "We thought he was immortal. An undead down on his luck."

Carla chortled. "Never did see him with kids or a wife. He never said why he wanted to sell. Just that he did."

"Carla," a young male approaching the table called out. She looked up, pushed back from the table, holding up a hand and rose.

"I need to talk with Stan before he signs in." Carla laid her napkin on the table and turned toward where Stan stood. She glanced back and added. "Good to see you and catch up a bit."

Carla walked a few steps away when the sound of a chair scraping against the floor caught her attention. A hand touched her shoulder. Need rolled through her like a pot of water ready to boil. She looked at the hand and raised her gaze. Kirk stood beside her, his other hand reaching toward her.

"We'd like to talk with you more." Kirk lowered his hand from her shoulder. "Daniel and I have a proposition for you."

Carla pressed her lips together. Kirk held his hand out to her. He added one more thing. "Please?"

Both of their kisses had touched her in ways she hadn't felt in quite a while. Spending more time with them wouldn't detract from her evening. An evening binge-watching reruns of old television shows paled the more she let her feelings talk. What could more talk hurt? Both of them sought her out and apparently wanted to spend more time with her. She wet her lips and spoke. "I've got to fill Stan in before he starts. That'll take fifteen to twenty minutes. If you're still here when I'm done, catching up more sounds like fun."

Kirk took hold of her hand, entwining his fingers with hers. He leaned close and brushed his lips over hers. He spoke as he pulled back. "Good. Thank you. And you look delicious. Hope you taste that good, too."

Kirk let go and walked away. Carla glanced at Daniel who waved and went back to studying the dessert menu. Carla turned and forced herself to walk back to the bar where Stan awaited her. Why had Kirk chosen that line? The thing he said two nights before her parents practically kidnapped her and moved them out of town. Almost the same exact thing Daniel had told her during their date that afternoon. Each had said they desired her and wanted to know her answer-would she have sex with them. Fucking wasn't what any of them had in mind. They got and understood their connection. They'd been ready to take it to another level. She'd never gotten the chance to respond to their question.

CHAPTER THREE

Carla kept walking, not looking back. Maybe Kirk didn't remember he said that line. Daniel hadn't voiced if his mind went there as they kissed. She put her hands palms down on the bar, needing the distraction to pull her out of the past and back into the here and now. She blinked, nodded, and smiled as she inhaled. Stan walked toward her as he tied his apron.

"Okay, boss. Ready for duty." Stan returned her smile as he reached the end of the bar.

"You eat? You still got time." Carla looked at her watch. "You're early."

Stan rubbed his stomach. "Oh, yes I ate. Fresh chicken salad with plum tomatoes, apple chunks, homemade mayo and wilted arugula with sweet sesame dressing. And a yeast roll fresh out of the oven drizzled with orange blossom honey butter."

"Damn, Chef Rory feeds you better than me. I got the special. How'd you rate that?" Carla moved behind Stan, reaching for the tablet she'd made notes on earlier.

Stan chuckled, leaned close, and pulled a small black square box out of his jeans pocket. He opened it and showed her the inside. It was empty. She could make out where a ring would sit if one occupied the box.

Carla looked up. Stan nodded. "Yup, I did it. Two days ago, to be exact."

"Chef Rory said yes?"

"Better than that. Served me a special meal complete with my favorite wine."

Carla opened her mouth. Stan held up his hand. "Let me finish."

She nodded.

"And then he refused to talk about it. Rory kept changing the subject until I finished eating."

"You're telling me he didn't answer you?"

"Picked up my plate. Shoved the paper under it at me. He looked at me and grinned. I unfolded the sheet and started laughing."

Carla frowned, shook her head and stared at Stan. Stan snickered and pulled a folded sheet of paper from his pocket. "Open it."

Carla unfolded the sheet, looked down and laughed. A heart with Stan and Chef Rory's name on it took up the top portion. Next, a plus symbol and a cake with the yes on it took up the rest of the sheet. She refolded the paper and handed it back to Stan. "What happened to the ring?"

"On a chain around his neck. He doesn't want to lose it or deal with cleaning it after cooking." Stan added, "Didn't know getting engaged amounted to a lot of drama."

Carla put her hand over her mouth. Stan shrugged and pointed to the tablet on the bar. She nodded, pulling the tablet to her. "I'm taking a few days off. Payroll's done. Stock order comes in Thursday. You're in charge."

Stan chuckled. "Okay, Rory's gonna love that."

Carla shook her head again. "See if the two of you can keep the volume down when you do spat. Don't want to run customers off."

Stan saluted her and moved off to take a customer's order.

Carla moved the tablet closer to the cash register where Stan would see it. She untied her apron, folded it and put it in the cubby hole under the register. She grabbed her jacket off the coat hooks in the alcove next to the bar as she clocked out. She needed one last item, her fanny pack, which was in her office near the front door. As she made her way back to where Kirk and Daniel sat, she started grinning. Inviting them into her office would cause chatter. Let it happen. She hadn't caused a ruckus in a while. Besides, a little chaotic fun without magic or supernatural overtones wasn't going to hurt anyone. Just give folks something to chatter about. Not that many of them bothered with gossip or read the local freebie newspaper with any regularity.

Daniel looked at his watch. "Do you think we should hold her to what she said?"

Kirk smirked. "Give her a few more minutes. I didn't read any discoloration to her aura. Red and golden as I remember. She kissed both of us pretty thoroughly."

"She sure did. I almost had to reach down and adjust my pants after I sat down. Hard on that didn't want to quit." Daniel pushed his empty dessert plate away. He drank the remainder of his water.

"Me too. Carla puts herself into a kiss. She focuses on you and you alone." Kirk bit into the last half of his and Daniel's shared dessert.

"Operation courtship is off with a bang. Now what?" Daniel asked.

"Isn't that a question we need to ask Carla?" Kirk stuffed the last bite of cheesecake into his mouth and chewed.

"Do we come right out and ask or wait to see what she says?"

Kirk shook his head. "Been a while since you dated?"

"Oh, hell yes! After I got the text from Sandy telling me she eloped with her best friend, I decided to take me out of the dating pool."

"I told Carla we had a proposition for her. She grinned and walked away after agreeing to talk with us more." Kirk swallowed part of his water.

"Okay, I guess we're moving forward then." Daniel pointed to his watch. "Twenty minutes are up."

Kirk looked out across the dining area and nodded. "Here she comes."

Carla reached the table as Daniel stood up. "Sorry it took a bit longer. I'm off and available."

"Uhm, dare I ask how available?" Daniel teased, moving up beside her.

"I'll answer that in a few. Come with me. My office is near the front and we can talk in there while I get my fanny pack and car keys." Carla faced Kirk. "That includes you, too."

Carla did an about-face and started back toward the bar area. She hesitated midway back, glancing over her shoulder. Daniel followed with Kirk behind him. Each had their jacket over their arms. A few women stepped in their path. Daniel shook his head and moved around them. Kirk did the same. Carla pressed her lips together. Grinning from ear to ear, leading the way to her office with two hot hunks trailing her—well, that wasn't what she'd anticipated, but she was doing it.

Carla waited in front of the door-marked office until Daniel and Kirk caught up with her.

"Still catching the trailers, I see," she teased, opening her office door.

"Something about not interested seems to ignite their curiosity even if I say nothing," Daniel countered, moving past her into the office.

Kirk winked as he entered past her. Carla entered her office, swiftly closing the door with a hard bang. She burst out laughing as she faced Daniel and Kirk. "I'm sure there's a bunch of questions going down. Eva waved at me as I came back to get you."

Daniel dropped into the chair closest to her desk, groaning. "Shit. Aunt Zelda and Aunt Naomi are going to want to know details."

Kirk sat next to Daniel. "We ain't gonna share more than what's necessary."

"You know how bullheaded they can be. I bet we're going to get the silent treatment regardless."

Carla sat in her desk chair, opened the right-hand lower drawer and took out her fanny pack. She unzipped it, reaching inside for her keys. "I'm sure we'll come up with something that will shut them up."

Daniel rolled his eyes. Kirk snorted. She chuckled and tossed her keys on the desk next to her pack. "So what's your proposition?"

Kirk glanced at Daniel who shrugged and nodded. Kirk smiled, reached up and patted Daniel's shoulder. "Never knew you for a loss of words."

"Sometimes they fail me."

Carla laughed. "Like the time I walked up to you on the bus, kissed you on the lips, and walked to the back of the bus."

"Could be," Daniel said, leaning back in his chair.

Kirk cleared his throat as he stood. He walked behind his chair. Leaning on the back, he faced her. "Remember our joint make-out session?"

Carla felt warmth start at the base of her neck and rush over her. Oh, did she remember it. Daniel and Kirk pressing their lips against her bare shoulders. Whispers about she wore a tube top to temp them. Nibbles up and down her neck until each worried her earlobes. And...

"From your flush and look, I'd say you do," Daniel offered.

"So what if I do?" Carla reached below the desk where neither Daniel nor Kirk could see her hand. She bunched and pulled the hem of her top loose from her jeans and plucked the top sending wafts of air upward. Their gazes took on almost the same intense look as then. She met their gazes. No looking away this time, breaking off the energy building between them. The heat then was nothing compared to what washed over her now. Then she thought she had time. Time to think. Time to consider what she wanted and the prospect of both of them pursuing her. Thanks to her parents and their purist viewpoints, she had it all taken away from her.

"It tells me I've got your attention," Kirk whispered in a low warm tone, leaning toward her.

Carla blinked, nodded and said. "Oh, you do."

Daniel chuckled. "Good, 'cuz that means we won't need to repeat the offer, will we?"

He blew her a kiss and looked at Kirk. "I think we've got her attention."

Kirk stepped away from the chair, talking as he moved toward her. "We're adults now. No parents, no school authorities. Nothing to keep us from taking things to the next level."

"Yes, only the three of us deciding where we go this time," Daniel added, walking around the desk. Stopping as he reached her opposite side.

Kirk closed the distance between them, reaching for her hand. Daniel took her other in his. He leaned down and kissed her cheek, his breath warming her ear. Kirk kissed her other cheek, speaking as he pulled back. "I want you."

"Yes, I want you too," Daniel said, cupping her cheek.

Carla glanced at Daniel. Then at Kirk. Both nodded, pushing her chair back until they squatted down in front of her, each holding out their free hand.

"We want to court you," Daniel and Kirk said in unison.

Carla rocked back, holding her hands up in the air. She tried to move. Her chair banged against the wall. She'd dreamt of this as a teen, fantasized about it in her hormone lust-filled masturbation moments, but to have it happening real time—that was another thing. "You want to what?"

"Court you," Daniel and Kirk replied.

"Why?" she asked, trying to move past Daniel and Kirk. There wasn't room to step around them or ease by without touching one or the other, if not both of them. Up to now, a kiss, a hug, and some memories were all she could muster. Touching them, surrounded by them, or meeting their gazes enveloped her in a web she—she what? Trying to breathe deeply took more focus than her mind could muster. Short, shallow panic breaths forced air into her lungs and fed the angst-filled panic waiting to explode.

Daniel knew that look. It had happened when he and Kirk had suggested dating both of them in high school. Carla had joked about having two hunks interested in her. The familiar refrain came up with their jokes and antics about who they were attracted to and what couples seemed to be striving for the top couple spot that changed every semester. Oh, the wide eyes and the darting glances while moving away or trying to escape. Yeah, he knew that look. The one that said give me space and do it now.

He moved to his left, creating space between Carla and him. He remembered her cousins locking her in the family broom closet with their magical brooms. Forty minutes of brushes, taps, and voices talking at her in languages she couldn't understand and magic she couldn't defend herself against. He couldn't blame her. Welding magic and translating at the same time took talent. A talent he'd only seen a few get command of. He stepped toward Carla, holding his hand out. "Carla, it's okay. Kirk and I want to court you. Not scare you or force you into saying yes."

Kirk leaned back against the desk, holding his hands up in front of him. "Take a couple deep breaths. I want you. Want you badly. Not at the expense of you feeling coerced into it."

Daniel took hold of the chair and pulled it out from behind Carla. He positioned the chair between them. This left an opening she could easily move through without touching him or Kirk.

"Thank you," Carla voiced, quickly moving out from behind the desk. "Cramped spaces give me the heebie-jeebies."

Daniel pushed the chair away from him as he spoke. "Are you okay? I remembered the broom closet incident."

Carla hugged herself. He pressed his lips together. Damn, he and Kirk should have. . .the past was over. Nothing could change it. The here and now gave them a second chance. Would Carla agree to give them a second chance?

"Yes, I'm okay. That memory rushes up to haunt me from time to time." Carla pulled the chair he sat in earlier away from the desk until there was ample open space between them. She dropped into the chair, chafing her arms.

"I understand," Daniel said, pushing the desk chair around the desk. He sat in it. "Sorry that happened."

"Man, Carla," Kirk began sitting in the chair he sat in before. "I'm sorry that happened."

Carla stopped rubbing her arms, looked up at them, and weakly smiled. "Neither of you are at fault. Caught me off guard. I still want to know why."

Daniel leaned forward, resting his elbows on his thighs. "I know a good thing when I see it. I had a good thing in high school. Want a chance at it again."

"Same here," Kirk added.

Carla looked at Kirk. His smile reached his eyes. He'd taught her that when a smile didn't reach a person's eyes, don't trust them. She glanced at Daniel. He puckered his lips and blew her a kiss. He grinned and nodded. He taught her to trust herself. Listen to her inner voice and heart. She raised her gaze until it met Daniel's. His eyes glowed as he blew her a second kiss. She took a deep breath, dropped her gaze and asked the question echoing in her head. "What if it doesn't work out this time either?"

Daniel snorted. "We didn't get a chance to see if it would before."

Kirk rose and walked over to her. He squatted close to her. "There's something you need to know."

Carla nodded, looking Kirk straight in the eye. "What's that?"

CHAPTER FOUR

"We," Kirk began, pointing to Daniel and him, "are in charge."

Carla looked at Daniel, who nodded in agreement. "Yes, we're Cauldron Falls' newest co-alphas."

Carla pressed her lips together, hoping her mouth didn't drop open. She'd heard Uncle Zac, as most referred to him, had retired. She didn't realize how close to home this hit. Hell, this upped the ante in a way she wasn't sure they understood. "Congrats. You sure you want to court me?"

"Yes," Daniel and Kirk responded. "Why not?"

"I ain't got no magic," Carla said, looking at both of them. Let that sink in and see what their answer was.

Kirk moved away from her first. She gripped the chair arms tighter to the point she could feel the edges of the arms pressing against her palms. She glanced at Daniel. He'd withdrawn his offered hand. Here it was again. The huge wedge driven between her and anyone magical or supernatural. The nagging refrain her parents, and magical medical practitioners pulled out every time she failed at performing a trick.

Daniel stood, moving into her line of vision where she could see him without having to glance sideways. He pointed at Kirk and him asking, "Why would that matter to us?"

"You're magics. Supernaturals. I'm not." Carla perched on the edge of her desk. "Purity of lineage and all that crap. You know, keep things clean and clear to trace who is what."

Daniel shook his head. "I'm going to point out the obvious here. Kirk and I are different species. Uncle Zac told the United Council he was naming his successors. Not a successor. The council agreed mixed leadership was needed. The future way things were going to be. Someone had to be the first. Uncle Zac took that chance with Kirk and I."

Kirk moved closer to Daniel. "One person leading was great when supernatural packs or magical groupings were small. After the Great Reveal, well we all need each other. It takes all of us to thrive and shine."

"Yeah, tell my parents that. The witches' council labeled me and others like me abominations. Not easy to shrug off that label and the outcast shit they put me through." Carla pushed off the desk. "Sorry. Neither of you did any of that to me."

"No we didn't. I know we've each had our share of heartbreak and crap to put up with." Daniel reached for her jacket. "How about we continue this discussion somewhere else?"

"Where?" Carla grabbed her jacket. "My trust meter is on no way."

Kirk pushed the chairs aside. "I feel ya. Your aura is flashing dark blue and green. Protection energy happening."

"Trusting what I can't see or know is real damn hard for me." Carla slipped her jacket on. "No reflection on either of you. I've done a flip-flop from out there to in here."

Daniel handed her her fanny pack. "Your world flipped in turn. You didn't expect us to show up. Or pursue you either."

"True. I took over Maxson's and charged full throttle ahead." Carla fastened her fanny pack around her waist. "Maybe it's time I slowed down and decide what comes next."

Kirk zipped up his jacket. "Let me handle Aunt Naomi and Aunt Zelda. I'll drop off a quick note signed by us stating we consent to courting each other should suffice."

"Best add we aren't answering questions or phones for the next couple of days either." Daniel started opening desk drawers. "Carla, where do I find pen and paper?"

Carla pushed the drawers shut Daniel hastily opened. "*My desk*. Move out of the way."

Daniel backed up, holding his hands up. "Blinders on. I apologize."

"Two steadfast rules I've got when it comes to Maxson's and my office. You don't assume. No making asses out of you and me. Plus don't fuck with things—my office and desk." Carla tossed a legal pad and two pens on the desk. "It took me three months to clear out Mr. Maxson's stuff and get his fucked up ledgers straight."

Kirk pulled the pad to him and picked up a pen. "Thanks for sharing. Mr. Maxson was a great businessman to a point. Bookkeeping and organization weren't his strong suits. Most knew his wife, Twyla, was the silent partner that kept things straight."

"Aren't we stirring up trouble with consenting to court each other?" Daniel read over Kirk's shoulder as he wrote. "You and I aren't interested in each other beyond friendship."

"Keeps em wondering." Kirk looked up and grinned. "Read it aloud."

Daniel pulled the pad to him. "Carla, Daniel and Kirk agree to a mutual courtship of Carla for an unspecified time period. By signing this agreement, Carla is on board for the courtship by Daniel and Kirk. Daniel and Kirk understand that Carla is courting both and each of them as well. The matchmakers recording this agreement will be notified if anything changes."

Carla pointed at the last line, reading it aloud. "This extends to no calls, email, texts, or any attempts to gather more information for the next seventy-two hours."

"Do you really think that is going to keep Aunt Naomi and Aunt Zelda from hounding us?" Daniel signed and printed his name and Co-Alpha Cauldron Falls Mixed Pack below his signature.

"It'll keep them wondering and muttering for sure. You added your power punch." Kirk grinned, signing next to Daniel's signature and adding his title as well. "Little extra tweak never hurts."

"You know Eva might not abide by this." Carla sighed, taking the pen from Kirk.

"She has to as a matchmaker apprentice witnessing a formal courtship declaration. Besides shouldn't your days off be peaceful and quiet? What you do only those involved need to know, right?" Kirk pointed to him and Daniel.

Carla quickly signed, printing her name and sole owner and proprietor under her signature. "Let your aunts and Eva ponder that one."

Kirk tore the sheet off the pad. "Do we need a copy of this?"

"Each of us takes a picture with our phone. That way we've each got a copy." Daniel took his picture first. Carla next and Kirk last.

Kirk folded the paper in half. "I'll meet you at Sadie's. Tonight's patio firepit night. Smores fixins. Hot apple cider. And Pierre and Chef's grilled ham and cheese rollups. Nice night to have mulled cider and a couple of hot snacks."

Daniel chuckled as Kirk exited the office. "He eats like he's seventeen and still growing."

Carla pulled her keys out of her jeans pocket. "I've heard shapeshifters eat for two and burn it off as quickly, too."

"Yeah. Us magics still got to watch our figure." Daniel spun around and faced Carla. "Come on, I'll walk you to your car. That way we can follow each other to Sadie's."

Carla slowed for the traffic light close to Main Street. Daniel was two car lengths ahead of her. Halfway through Maxson's parking lot, he'd turned and swept her into his arms. A quick, tight hug as he whispered that Eva watched them. Carla tried to turn and see where Eva was. Daniel loosened his embrace advising that Eva had gone back inside. Doubt had reared its ugly head along with uneasiness until they reached her car. Daniel's mid-sized compact sat two parking spaces over. He joked how the metallic red stood out in the daylight and not so great in the dark. He waited until she was inside her vehicle and the motor running before he trotted over to his car and got in. She knew the way to Sadie's. Siobhan had told her about Mr. Maxson looking for a buyer and wanting to retire. Praise deities, tonight wasn't a full moon. No Sadie Hawkins thirty-day match time limit. Carla wondered how long it had taken Kirk to get away from his and Daniel's aunts.

Kirk turned the music down as Daniel exited his car. Two alphas driving a pick-up truck and a mid-sized compact. Who'd believe it? Uncle Zac and his great nephew Caleb challenged them to do away with societal expectations and lead as cohorts and equals. Caleb's wife Maggie's delivery date was two and a half months out. Change wasn't a what-if anymore. Cauldron Falls and Sylvan Valley populace were a mixture. Mixture of magics, mortals and supernaturals that blended together forming a diverse citizenry. Kirk turned the radio and the truck off. "You made good time."

"I didn't expect you to beat us here." Daniel pointed to Carla's car turning into the parking lot. "Eva came out looking for Carla. You must have gotten an earful for that to happen."

"Nah. I walked up to the table, dropped the paper, waited long enough for Aunt Naomi to skim it, and said you've got your consent form and left." Kirk shut the truck's door and locked it. "Eva kept calling my name as I walked out. Probably missed you and Carla as I ducked and darted through the parking lot."

Daniel chortled. "We're going to get an earful when and if we answer our phones."

"I got two texts and a call from Eva demanding to know what happened." Carla walked up beside them. "It felt good to let the call roll to voice mail.

Thank you for sweeping me away as Eva called. Time off is good for the boss. Playtime is as well."

Daniel flanked Carla on one side. Kirk on Carla's other. Each held out their hands. Carla clasped theirs with hers. Three abreast, they made their way across the parking lot and entered the patio area near the rear of Sadie's loading dock.

Siobhan rose, Ty's hand on the small of her back, steadying her. "Carla, great to see you. I thought you'd be at Maxson's till closing."

"Who told me even owners need time off?" Carla embraced Siobhan and stepped back. Carla laid her hand on Siobhan's stomach. Three ripples rushed across her palm. "Are the triplets behaving?"

"Laine, Ruth, and Arthur are night owls. Like their parents." Ty hugged Carla. "How are you doing?"

"Ty, good to see you. I'm doing well." Carla turned to Kirk and Daniel. "I'd like to introduce my courting matches, Daniel and Kirk."

"Courting matches?" Siobhan held out her hand. "Daniel, nice to meet you. Kirk, the same."

"Uncle Zac retired. Made us co-alphas." Daniel shook Siobhan and Ty's hands.

"Pleasure to meet you, Siobhan and Ty." Kirk shook hands. "Congratulations on the triplets. Going to have your hands full."

Siobhan laughed. "Lots of things full. I'm glad Carla's taking some time off."

"I'm trying it." Carla sat on the bench close to the fire in the fire pit. "Is there any food and drink available?"

"Nathan, the new barkeep, just went inside to get refills for us. Most patrons are inside milling. A few ventured out. Off full moon night match chances happening." Ty filled three cups with cider and handed them to Carla, Daniel and Kirk. "What brings you here?"

Daniel sat next to Carla. He sipped his cider. "Good cider. Trying to talk without ears around. Aunt Naomi and Aunt Zelda."

Siobhan grinned. "The Sister Three gets around. Tara is here tonight. My Aunt Elana and James would be too except they're honeymooning."

"Sounds like your family's been busy." Carla wrapped her hands around her glass of cider. "I'd appreciate you keeping our being here between us. Eva's mothering radar was blaring loudly as Daniel and I tried to get away."

"More than loudly." Kirk pulled up a chair from the table close to the benches and sat in it. "She kept calling out my name after I dropped our note on the table. I ignored her and kept walking."

"No wonder she was outside scanning the parking lot." Carla drank most of her cider. "Whoa, that's partly hardened!"

"Fermented and still aging." Siobhan smiled. "Figured you could use a jolt."

Daniel groaned. "How so?"

Kirk snorted. "Some of us sober quicker than others. Carla possibly not."

Ty held up the bottle. "That is the last of it. Siobhan and I toasted each other with a couple of sips before you got here. We finally decided on the triplets' names."

"Congratulations." Kirk down the last of his cider. "Non-fermented for me going forward. I'm driving."

"Me too." Daniel drank the rest of his cider.

"I think I need some coffee or plenty of water after that." Carla handed her glass to Ty. "I'm the one that doesn't sober fast."

"Got ya." Ty set the glasses on the tray on the servicing table. "Don't need you picked up for drunk driving."

"You could come home with Ty and me. Let Daniel and Kirk fend for themselves." Siobhan whistled a ditty and looked away.

"Gee, thanks!" Kirk pulled a chair up next to him. "Siobhan and Ty, you're welcome to join our conversation."

Siobhan sat next to Kirk. Ty sat on the bench close to Daniel. "How can we help?"

"Non-full moon and not Sadie Hawkins matches fall outside matchmaking norms." Daniel held up a hand. "I smell food and smores makings."

Siobhan turned. "Nathan, thank you for bringing these. We need a pot of decaf coffee and five mugs."

"Cream, sugar, and spoons too." Ty set the tray and cider glasses on the empty tray Nathan held. "Thanks for keeping an eye out. If anyone asks where Siobhan or I are, we're not to be disturbed."

Nathan started to step away and turned back. "Patrons are thinning out inside. Forty-five minutes till closing."

CHAPTER FIVE

Carla picked up two grilled ham and cheese roll-ups. "I'm going to be blunt. Daniel, Kirk and I need some place to talk things out. Time to move past our past and into the here and now. Hope that makes sense."

"It does. Ty and I needed almost the same thing when we found out about the triplets. Working and talking things through can take time and knowing you got the safe space to do it matters." Siobhan entwined her fingers with Ty's.

"How can we help?" Ty blew Siobhan a kiss.

"Triad and quad pair bondings are not unusual. What's unique about ours is two alphas, co-alphas and a non-magic forming it." Daniel broke a grilled ham and cheese roll in half, popped one half in his mouth and chewed.

"Do you know somewhere we can merge into the crowd? Have the space, privacy and time to find us?" Kirk glanced at his watch. "Don't want to keep you past closing."

"Don't worry." Ty glanced toward Sadie's back door as Nathan exited carrying a tray with a coffee carafe and mugs on it. "We've got time. Nathan is good about last call and checking in with Siobhan before he leaves."

"Take your time. Ty and I understand where you're coming from. We needed time to plan us. Thinking out loud and talking with Aunt Elana and James helped some. Everyone has opinions and suggestions." Siobhan took the tray from Nathan. "Thank you, Nathan."

"Welcome, Siobhan." Nathan faced Daniel. "My cousin, Whitney, isn't going to be able to paint and decorate your place. She and her girlfriend eloped last night."

Daniel sighed. "Thanks Nathan. I thought something was up when Whitney didn't email the contract or the list of items we discussed at our last meeting."

"I just got the text. My phone service has been up and down all day. She recommended several other interior decorators in the email she sent you."

"It's all right. I haven't paid attention to email for several days. Been busy with the reunion committee and pack council business." Daniel stood. "I'll check them out. Don't worry Nathan, Whitney told me she wasn't sure she could get to me before she got hitched."

26

Nathan grinned. "Hitched and out of business. I bet *neither of us* expected that one."

"Sure didn't." Daniel poured coffee into each of the mugs. He creamed and sugared his. He started to stir his coffee. He stopped, turned around and pointed to Nathan. "Thank you! I know where Kirk, Carla and I can hide out."

Kirk groaned. "Carla, how good are you at painting?"

Carla sipped her coffee. "Depends on what you want painted. By numbers, decent. Walls not so great. Priming is about my best there is. Main question is, how much painting Daniel are you planning on us doing?"

"Strip off wallpaper and touch up paint for now. One room at a time." Daniel sat on the bench, holding his mug and a smore. "No one expects me to be there during this. Park in the garage. No one knows we're there."

Kirk finished his smore and coffee. "How about this? We each go home tonight and pack. One of us picks Carla up and we meet up at your place tomorrow early."

"Eva may be waiting for me at my place." Carla set her empty mug on the tray. She yawned and stretched. "I'll text her me and Daniel don't need chaperoning. She did see us leave together."

"How about this? I follow you to your house." Daniel glanced at his watch. "If Eva is watching, she is night owling, we can turn a few lights on and off especially in your bedroom if it's got a front window. You gather up a few things for painting clothes and otherwise. We come out, get in my car and head off."

"I can meet you at Daniel's. I can pull through the garage and park in the back carport." Kirk stood and stretched. "Gotta gather my painting clothes too."

"Kirk, you go ahead. You left before Daniel and me." Carla wrapped her smore in several napkins and started to put it in her jacket pocket. "Daniel, it's better if I follow you to your place in my car. That way the consent part of all this stays lucrative and visible."

"Let me get you something better to wrap your smore in. Possibly a box of them. Chef and Pierre probably have leftovers. They'd love to send you home with roll-ups and smores." Siobhan started making her way toward Sadie's back entrance. "Ty will bring them out to you. I've got closing things to attend to."

Ty motioned Daniel, Kirk and Carla to him. "Siobhan's baby shower is in three weeks. I'm inviting folks via word of mouth cuz her aunt, James and I, along with a few of her siblings, want to surprise her. We've got about forty-five RSVPs. You can contribute a gift card or two if you like. There's a couple of indie baby shops in Sylvan Valley and Cauldron Falls, we're registered with."

"Where are you holding it?" Carla asked, watching Siobhan make her way up the steps at the end of the patio. "You can use Maxson's banquet room. Just let me know the date and time. We'll take care of the catering, too."

Ty hastily entered Maxson's phone number into his phone. "Appreciate it, Carla. Thanks a lot. Keeping this on the Q.T. hasn't been easy. Can I get you the info next week?"

"Leave a message with Stan, my assistant bartender. He'll get the info to me." Carla nodded toward Sadie's exit. "Siobhan is watching us. Go get the stuff from Chef and Pierre. We'll wait right here."

Carla caught Ty's quick thumb up as he turned and trotted to where Siobhan waited. Ty and Siobhan made their way inside. As the door closed, Carla faced Daniel and Kirk. "We've gone into the party planning business, gents. Painters, party planners, and dodge and duck artists. Quick change artists part of tonight's learning experience, too."

Kirk fished his car keys out of his pocket. "I need about fifteen minutes to get things together. It's twenty minutes to my place from here. Thirty back to Daniel's."

"Carla, think we can kill an hour at your place?" Daniel grinned as he added, "Turn lots of lights on and off. Sit in the dark for a bit. *And what else?*"

"That I don't need to know," Kirk said, walking toward the patio exit gate. "TMI is a word I prefer to not use. I don't need to know what position, where, when or how."

"I don't do and tell either," Carla added, walking toward Sadie's back entrance. "Asking isn't going to work either."

Daniel glanced at Kirk as he exited, back at Carla moving to where Ty stood holding a box and bag. He didn't know what was worse. Kirk's sarcastic sense of humor. Or Carla's ironic replies. Daniel shook his head as he made his way to Carla and Ty. Either way, looked like dull moments with this triad weren't going to happen.

"Thanks Ty." Carla took the bag. "What's in the box?"

"Breakfast croissants. Ham, egg and cheese. Chef finished up his breakfast baking. Pierre added in some of his special breakfast coffee." Ty pointed to the bag. "A dozen smores. Siobhan added two quarts of her homemade yogurt."

"You'd think we were hiding out in the woods with all this food." Carla looked in the bag. "Fresh fruit, too?"

"Never know when a good snack in between painting walls can come in handy." Ty winked. "Best of luck with painting. Text me if you need anything. My phone number is on the card inside the box. Eva isn't going to suspect me dropping stuff off at Daniel's. She's never met me."

Daniel coughed. "Enough already. If Eva is being that nosey, it's time Aunt Naomi and Aunt Zelda give her the mind-your-own business matchmaker talk. Aka, they either work it out or they don't."

"Wish more folks followed that advice." Ty hugged Carla. "Siobhan is waiting for me to help her finish up the night's bank receipts. Be safe. Be careful. Good luck."

Daniel moved closer to Carla as Ty trotted up the steps and entered Sadie's. "Careful and safe. Lucky. I think we've got a start on each of those."

"Possibly we do. There's still stuff we gotta talk out." Carla started toward the patio exit. "Painting and talking. Fussing and cussing. Hopefully there's no paint throwing unless you want psychedelic tie-dyed colored walls."

Daniel pressed his lips together hoping to quell his mirth. How any of them kept a straight face was beyond him. Fussing and cussing he could handle. Painting and talking, too. But psychedelic tie-dye colored walls. . .not happening. Neon colors gave him vertigo worse than when he spun around on the elementary school merry-go-round as a kid. Puking non-stop for ten minutes and laying on the floor wondering when it would stop spinning was not how he wanted to spend minutes and hours, much less days and weeks with his triad partners. He followed Carla out the gate and latched it.

"Question I should have asked back at Maxson's." Daniel stopped as they reached their cars. "Where's your place?"

"Think I'm going to deliberately get you lost?" Carla rocked back on her heels, tossing her keys in the air and catching them one-handed. "Not worth the time and effort. I bought Aunt Moriah's place. Close to Ye Woods Landing homes."

Daniel unlocked his car, set the smores box and leftover bag on his back seat and closed the door. "The development two packs fought city council about. The zoning committee left plenty of woods between the development and pack territories."

"Don't blame them for wanting to keep plenty of undeveloped areas. Some folks may not handle a half-wolf, half-human running through their backyard. Heard rumors of a few streaking about last full moon." Carla unlocked her car. "It'll take us twenty minutes to get there from here. Cross-town traffic is no issue this time of night."

"You lead. I'll follow. I hope you texted Eva. I don't like surprises." Daniel opened Carla's car door.

"I will once we're underway. Two long stop lights regardless of what hour it is. Long enough to send a text." Carla rocked forward on her tiptoes, pressed her lips to Daniel's and moved back. She quickly got in her car, shut the door, clicked the locks and started the engine.

Daniel trotted around his car and got in. Five minutes later, they pulled out of Sadie's parking lot.

Carla sent her text first of the two long traffic lights waiting to make the turn onto the parkway leading out of town toward Ye Woods Landing. Her phone chimed twice. She glanced at the caller ID at the next stop sign. *Eva*. Texts weren't even minutes apart. Seconds apart with a third one rolling in as Carla entered the traffic circle roundabout. Construction cones were up. Flashing signs and the bright overhead lights confirmed another night of pounding and the smell of asphalt and paint as the work crews widened Country Lane East to accommodate the influx of traffic off East-West Parkway.

Partway through the roundabout, Carla glanced in the rearview mirror. Daniel was two car lengths behind her. Twice, she thought she'd lost him. Ready to pull over and wait, Carla smiled as Daniel came up behind her flashing his car's high beams. An old signal they used to use following each other home after Friday night football games. Goddess on high, she wished her parents hadn't been so damn hardheaded. Genetics was genetics. Nothing could change the random chaos genetics tossed in from time to time. Two tremendous things resulted from her escape from Witchery and enrolling in Wichita University. She reunited with Eva and learned to be strong. Be herself. Comfortable in her own skin.

One more stop sign until she and Daniel were clear of the roundabout and on Woods Landing Lane. Carla grabbed her cell phone as Eva's assigned ring tone sounded. Carla touched no answer and tossed her cell phone on the center console. Halfway down Woods Landing Lane, she glanced at cars parked out front of her neighbors' homes. Eva's mid-size SUV wasn't among them. Carla loosened her grip on the steering wheel. She glanced down the two side streets close to her house. Nothing unusual. Maybe Eva stood down this time. Two more houses and . . .Carla turned into her driveway. A legal-sized white envelope on her garage door stood out against the car's headlights illuminating it. Daniel pulled in next to her.

CHAPTER SIX

"I see someone left you a message." Daniel pointed to the envelope attached to the garage door. "Reckon it's Eva?"

Carla looked around as she locked her car. "If it is, I hope she's in bed reading one of those thriller mysteries she's fond of."

"True Detective novels are not for the faint of heart." Daniel pulled the envelope off the garage door and handed it to Carla.

"From some of the so-called shapeshifter kid tales I've heard bits and pieces of, I'm pretty sure Eva isn't reading True Detective novels. Ghosts, magics and supernaturals doing stuff that is normal for you." Carla stuffed the envelope in her jacket pocket.

"Urban Fantasy is my preferred. Cross over into mortal realms while bits and pieces of our realness are thrown in." Daniel beeped his car locks.

"Kirk's fave reading?" Carla inserted her key into the front door lock.

"Sci-Fi and Fantasy. He excelled in hard science classes at the university. Why he chose a business degree is something I still don't get." Daniel stepped up beside her.

"I suppose everyone understands why you chose Art History with a Finance minor." Carla opened the door and took her key out of the lock.

"Cataloging art paid off while I toured Europe working for several of the major museums. Also got me a lucrative job tracking down missing pieces from shapeshifter and witch history." Daniel closed the door behind him as he followed her inside.

"General studies got me through till my senior year, and I had to declare a major of some sort to graduate. Hospitality management was the easiest way to piss my parents off and where I excelled with the credits I got for my work-study aid." Carla turned on the lamp on the end table closest to her. Bright light illuminated part of the room and the drawn front window curtains.

"Education is a plus. Doesn't matter what you major in as long as you're good at what you do. Me—I'm good at history, art design and seeing the larger picture. Kirk tried ROTC for a semester. Getting up early on his drill days was a pain. Friday night and in bed at ten cuts into your social life real quick." Daniel tossed his jacket on the arm of the chair closest to the door. He sat on the couch and patted the space next to him. "If we're being watched, let's give 'em a show."

Carla stared at him. "What show?"

Daniel laughed. "You sit next to me. I put my arm around you and you turn to face me. We'll lean into each other like we're making out. I can kiss you a couple of times so you don't have to lie."

Carla undid her fanny pack and set it on the end table next to the chair. She slipped her jacket off and laid it next to Daniel's. "Bullshitting Eva isn't easy. She reads auras like cookbooks. I guess a couple of quick kisses won't hurt. Don't want Kirk thinking we're pulling something over on him."

"We'll tell him what happened when we get to my place. Two quick kisses and we keep the lean into each other for a bit making it seem like the kiss is longer." Daniel laid his arm on the back of the couch.

Carla flexed her hands. Last time she kissed Daniel. . .heat enveloped them and damn near singed them. If Kirk hadn't announced his arrival as he climbed the treehouse ladder, clothes and passion would have littered the treehouse like shredded pieces of paper floating in the wind. Whirlwind that is.

"One thing, we can keep to the plan, right?" Carla sat next to Daniel.

Daniel nodded. "No lies between any of us. That is a key part of Kirk and my friendship. One of the reasons Uncle Zac said the packs needed co-alphas. The time had come for cooperative leadership instead of constant competition setting off ongoing arguments and further divisions among Cauldron Falls' supernatural and shapeshifter citizens."

"How about we open the envelope first?" Carla started to stand.

"What about the anticipation for whoever is waiting and watching?" Daniel leaned toward Carla, his lips puckered.

Carla walked over, turned the light off and sat on Daniel's lap. "Let them guess. Here's your kiss."

She brushed her lips over Daniel's. "Get ready for your second one."

Carla cupped Daniel's face. His breath mingled with hers. Sliding one hand lower, she lay against Daniel. "I'd forgotten how nice your arms around me feel."

"Memories serve reminders." Daniel looped his arms around her neck. "Reality delivers in the moment. Like now."

Daniel nipped her neck, kissing the spot he nipped. He continued making his way up her neck until he reached her earlobe. Suckling it between his teeth, he worried it briefly and let go. His hot breath rushed over her ear as he whispered, "No time to do what I'd like to do. Pleasure you. Watch you flush with ecstasy and desire as I . . ."

"As you wha. . ." Daniel's lips captured hers cutting off anything else she said.

His hands trailed down her arms, lingering near her breasts. He brushed his knuckles lightly across and over their sides. Daniel settled tighter to her. If their clothes weren't in the way. . . .images from her dreams and fantasies flashed across her closed lids. Each one more vivid than the prior.

Daniel parted his lips, tracing both of Carla's with his tongue. Savoring each taste, he pressed his lips tighter against Carla's. He wouldn't go any further unless she signaled him she was open to it.

Carla parted her lips. The tip of her tongue touched Daniel's. Sweet coffee, a hint of chocolate and the lingering heat of the chocolate cayenne pepper smores reached out tantalizing her. Urging her to follow deeper into the kiss. Daniel's arm slid around her tighter. His hand splayed across the middle of her back. He moved her closer to him. There was no mistaking his desire. Daniel's erection nudged her each time he moved. She ignited want and lust at the same time.

Tangling her fingers in Daniel's hair, Carla cradled his head, pressing her lips tight to his. Their tongues parlaying and twisting in the age-old mating dance french kiss.

Daniel pulled back, breaking off the kiss. "Stopping before we go somewhere we might be ready to go. Chemistry we got. Desire and need we got. Control we almost didn't."

Carla placed her hands on Daniel's shoulders, trying to rise. "This isn't going to be easy."

Daniel brushed his lips over hers, placed his hands on her waist, and lifted her slightly off his lap. "Not when my lower half wants to shuck clothes and rub slippery bits together."

"Mine are screaming no fair. My heart is pounding and my psyche is flashing red and green at me, hoping I'll give in."

"My inner mage is wanting us to mark our mate." Daniel hefted her onto the couch next to him. He stood. "I need to work a bit of this energy off. How about we go get a drink in the kitchen and get whatever foodstuff you want to take with?"

"See what's in the envelope?" Carla smoothed her hands down her jeans. Sweaty palms indicated. . .indicated what? Nervousness? Uncertainty? Fear? She turned and walked into the kitchen flexing her hands. Could she be that flexible in her decisions? In being in the moment? She sure as hell wasn't letting fear drive. Her parents did that when they swooped her and her siblings up to Witchery, Nevada. The hellish spot in the middle of the northern Nevada desert. Nearest large city was two and a half hours away. The weekly trip for food and supplies was arduous. Her parents relentless dogging her every step and keeping her tight to them. Carla inhaled, counting as she slowly exhaled. Envisioning her past going up in a bright yellowish-red flame. Keeping and staying calm required focus.

"Daniel, I need to share something before we go any further." Carla turned as she reached the counter. Daniel was close behind her. He stopped midway between her and the kitchen table littered with papers and receipts.

"Do I need to sit down?" Daniel reached for a chair.

"Not sure." Carla leaned against the counter. "I'm not as strong as you think I am. I've changed. Been through some shit that I can't always push away or keep out of my subconscious."

"Can any of us?" Daniel closed the space between them, holding out his hand as he did. "It took Kirk several months to stop looking over his shoulder his first few months in college. I couldn't stop pinching pennies and going over my bank statements twice until my sophomore year. We've all got ghosts of our own creation."

Carla looked down at Daniel's hand and back up. His gaze on her. "I'm not perfect. I'm not the Carla you knew in high school or in the tree house. I've changed."

"So have I. So has Kirk." Daniel took a step back. "Do you want me to leave?"

Carla shook her hands and reached toward Daniel. "No. Parts of who we are hasn't changed. Like you said, chemistry is there. I got that kissing Kirk."

"Good. Consent matters. If you are feeling cornered, pushed, or scared, *please* let Kirk and me know. We're in this together." Daniel clasped her hand, brushed his lips over her knuckles and turned her hand over palm up. He licked her palm, pressed his lips against her palm and curled her fingers into her palm. "Hold on to that. Know that regardless of how this courtship turns out, I am always your friend and here for you. We're family."

"Thanks. The same goes for you. Do I mark you like you did me?" Carla reached for Daniel's other hand. He held it up, palm toward her.

"You can mark me any way you like. The best way to keep your scent lingering on me is rubbing your sweat on me. Pheromones leave a mark." Daniel reached toward her.

"Problem is my pheromones are nerve-loaded and probably topped off with fear-laced injections." Carla held up her sweaty palm. "Don't think that is a great marker."

Daniel clasped her wrist, tugging her to him until she gripped him to keep her balance. "Marking done. No need to worry about what mix you marked me with. I'm marked. Remember you need to mark Kirk when we get to my place. He'll be able to tell I'm marked and claimed."

Carla shook her head. "What if I'm not ready to mark and claim either of you?"

"You already did kissing both of us hello as you did. Pheromones marked each of us when that happened. Excess marked Kirk and I with each other's pheromones from you touching each of us after you had touched each of us." Daniel kissed her cheek and let go.

"I don't know whether to kick, gut punch or beat the shit out of you. Both of you over that one." Carla pointed toward the living room. "Go get the envelope out of my jacket. Maybe some sanity will return between now and then."

"AKA you cooling off." Daniel blew her a kiss and sauntered away swinging his hips like he conquered her. "I'm cooling off too. Swaying hips creates a breeze over my balls and cock. No need to unzip my fly and drop my jeans, if you know what I mean."

Carla filled two glasses with ice water, set them on the table and placed a tin of homemade oatmeal raisin cookies between them. Daniel and Kirk's fave homemade cookies. One of the things her great aunt secretly passed to her on one of her clandestine visits. Aunt Moriah the family peacekeeper until her parents decided she would be better off in the old witches' home. Carla sat in the chair closest to her, rolled her eyes heavenward and offered a subdued incantation. "Thank you, Aunt Moriah. Thanks for the recipes. This house and for understanding me when the rest of the family scoffed at me for my lack of magical abilities. Thank you for showing me that magic entails many different and unique things. Unique ways of seeing, believing and abilities to do. Food and hospitality being mine. Love you always, Aunt Moriah. Thank you again for everything."

Warmth swept over her cheek, a soft whisper Carla swore was her aunt's voice saying she loved her too came and vanished as Daniel re-entered the kitchen. He held the envelope in one hand, his cell phone and her fanny pack in his other.

"According to Kirk's text he sent both of us, Eva isn't going to be around much." Daniel laid her fanny pack on the table.

"Oh?" Carla reached for her fanny pack.

"Yeah, seems she got a match. One she couldn't turn down." Daniel chuckled as he pushed his phone across the table to Carla. "Sebastien Stonehenge, heir to the Stonehenge royal family, claimed her."

"Eva kept telling me Sebastien was a royal pain in the ass. He kept telling her she was the one. He wasn't taking no for an answer."

"That is a tale I bet quite a few folks wanna hear. What Eva's reaction was when she found out her next-door neighbor is a royal prince from one of England's oldest magical realms." Daniel laid the envelope on the table. "Ready to see what the message inside is? Almost like a message in a bottle that washed up on the beach from who knows where."

CHAPTER SEVEN

Daniel pushed the envelope across the table to Carla. Carla fingered the edge of the envelope. The writing on the envelope didn't look familiar. Eva printed the first letter of everyone's name and cursively wrote the rest. Whoever wrote this printed each upper case letter with a firm stroke. Her name was easy to make out.

Carla pulled the envelope to her. "Did you pick up any energy from it? Any aura pulses?"

"Hard to do with inanimate objects." Daniel pointed to the envelope. "Don't know how long it was there. If there's any energy left, it's too faint for me to read."

Carla nodded. "I guess it's safe to open then. No weird spells or wardings waiting to latch on to either of us."

"I picked up your house's energy. The vibrations were and are harmonious. Don't be scared." Daniel rose and walked behind her. "Your great aunt lived here with you. I remember seeing her on the front porch of the house as a youth. She treated all of us the same. She baked cookies and sat on the front steps talking with us about school."

"Aunt Moriah held onto the farmland after Great Granddad passed. She kept the road passable and offered locals garden plots. Many humans learned canning and cooking from scratch from her. She deeded the last hundred and fifty acres to the city." Carla tore one end of the envelope open and pulled the paper inside out. She smoothed it out on the table, read part of it, and tipped her head back, grinning up at Daniel.

Daniel leaned forward, pointing to the signature. "Sebastian and Eva eloped? Seriously Sebastian? I bet he didn't tell her that part of heading to Sylvan Valley."

"Eva's going to meet her future in-laws without knowing it." Carla laughed. "Oh, that is going to be a fireworks-filled meeting. She kept dodging Sebastian and putting off taking the trip with him. He said he needed her to fake their involvement."

"This is going to be almost as infamous as Nick and Sandra's was." Daniel hugged Carla and returned to his chair. "Another story for another evening once they return."

"Agreed." Carla pushed the cookie tin to Daniel. "Homemade oatmeal raisin. A quick snack while we discuss what I'll need to pack."

Daniel reached for the tin. "Aunt Moriah's recipe?"

"Yes. The only recipe I use." Carla folded the paper and stuffed it back in the envelope. "Why would Sebastian leave me a note?"

Daniel held up a cookie. "One bite. Then I'll answer, okay?"

"Sure." Carla laid her cookie next to her glass. She handed Daniel a napkin. "I think Sebastian did it because he knows Eva would call me to come and get her."

Daniel chewed his bite of cookie, savoring the sweet brown sugar and raisin taste, and swallowed. He sipped his water and set the glass down. "Call you to the rescue? I thought Eva has more smarts than that."

"Not rescue her. Be her escape vehicle. A way back from wherever he's taking her." Carla popped a piece of her cookie into her mouth and chewed.

"Instead of what if, let's take this from what the note says. Sebastien planned the trip. He asked Eva to fake involvement. Why? We don't know except he felt she could pull it off." Daniel ate the rest of his cookie and finished his water. "Lupa help him if he lied to her."

"We'll take the rest of these with us. There's another tin in the cabinet we can take, too." Carla put the lid on the cookie tin. "Aunt Moriah told me more than once sometimes you don't know you found the one or ones until you've oopsed a few times."

Daniel put dish detergent in their glasses, filled them with water and rinsed them clear. He put them in the dish drainer as he continued speaking. "Wise woman. I can vouch for that. I've oopsed quite a few times. Until I decided to listen to my heart and hear what it was saying. Took a few times to get the translation right."

"My parents were too busy fighting and blaming each other since I got the weak human non-magic genes to quote my pain-in-the-ass parents." Carla got the second cookie tin out of the cabinet. "I didn't remember Aunt Moriah's advice until I was a few hundred miles removed from my family."

"I think we all had times we had to get away from family, find out who and what we were and are. Not a simple task when valuing yourself isn't taught or reinforced. Thankfully we had and have other family members who showed us by example." Daniel picked up the cookie tins. "Got a bag we can put these in?"

"Plastic grocery bag holder on back of the pantry door. Second door over next to the stove. Other door is the broom closet. No magical brooms or mops in it!" Carla dried their glasses and put them in the cabinet. She hung the dish towel on the rack next to the window.

Daniel grinned as he turned back toward Carla. "Aunt Naomi taught me one quick spell for pain in the ass enchanted brooms and mops."

"Oh? What's that?" Carla started toward the living room.

"Stop. Just stop right now." Daniel stepped into the pantry. His voice carried as he continued talking. "Stop your nonsense right now!"

Carla did a quick about-face, trotted over to the pantry door and flung it open. "Daniel, you can stop yelling at me. I heard you clearly. If you need help, ask."

Daniel stepped around the door, laughing. "You asked what the spell was. I answered you."

"That was the spell? Stop your nonsense right now?" Carla glared at him.

"Yup. Simple and direct. Assertive tone and keyword repeated three times. Different elements mixed with where it was said. You can say the statements in different order and keep the inanimate magic confused and spiraling inward on itself." Daniel placed the cookie tins in the bag. "Now you done in here?"

Carla looked down and back up. Her gaze met his. "Yes. I'm ready to pack my clothes and toiletries."

"I'll put this by our coats." Daniel exited the kitchen.

Carla glanced around her. Aunt Moriah was right. The kitchen was the focal point of the home. Problem was no family to gather around the table. Daniel and her at the table was the closest she'd come. Lingering memories of her friends and Aunt Moriah sitting around the table decorating holiday cookies, cutting out coupons for grocery runs and planning on who went where to get them, and the quiet moments she and Aunt Moriah shared sitting basking in the morning sun beaming through the kitchen window illuminating the table and them. Carla blinked, wiped a tear off her cheek and moved forward. "Aunt Moriah, thank you for making this a home. Thank you for showing me how to make this my home with you. I wish we'd had more time together once I came back to Cauldron Falls."

Carla took another step forward. Ringing sounded in her right ear, then her left. Growing in pitch as the kitchen faded from view. Words formed on the whiteboard in front of her.

My dear niece, I'm always here for you. Light the candle and round it three times circle right to left, then left to right. Invoke your personal magic. It's there waiting for you to tap into it. Call me to you and I will appear.

Carla swallowed hard, tugged her earlobe and blinked. The high-pitched ringing stopped as her mind cleared. "Aunt Moriah, I have no magic. I can't do tricks. My incantations make no sense."

"You talking to me?" Daniel entered the kitchen. "I'm sorry I missed part of what you said."

"How about talking to myself?" Carla stepped away from Daniel. "Come on, I'll grab my stuff and we'll go."

Daniel sniffed the air once. Twice. Laying his hand on her arm as he spoke. "I smell Aunt Moriah's perfume."

"Huh?" Carla pressed her lips together. She slowly inhaled. Aunt Moriah's perfume? Sweet Vanilla Verbena? Couldn't be.

"Aunt Moriah's perfume lingers in the air. I know it's not you. I've smelled you up close twice tonight." Daniel slid his hand down her arm as he faced her. "She was here. You summoned the portal that separates our realm from the next. The hereafter."

"But how?" Carla moved further away from Daniel. She chafed her arms, looking around the kitchen again. "I'm not a magic."

"We all have a bit of magic in us. Even humans. Kirk manifests itself in his shapeshifter dual nature. Mine with my male witchness. We live our lives with our dual counterparts. Human magic, AKA personal magic, shows up in ways that are distinctive to humans. Like being good at cooking. Math. Or even caring for others like medical personnel do." Daniel held out his hand. "It's recognizing that and understanding what is special about each of us that is the connection."

Carla let go a sigh. Relief washed over her. "I've sensed spirits and heard them from time to time since I was a teen. Does that make me a witch? A magical?"

"It makes you, you. Carla, the person who understands Kirk and me. Cares about others. Does hospitality management because it allows you to take care of and nurture others through offering them a hot meal, a job and often a place to find solace for a few moments while they breathe and consume food and drink." Daniel squeezed her hand. "You're special. Unique and rare. One of the reasons I cherish and treasure you."

Daniel mouthed something more as he turned. She couldn't read his lips. His whispered response she barely caught pieces of. Had he said the L word? Love? How could he? They barely knew each other beyond their shared past.

"Daniel," Carla called, exiting the kitchen. He was already partway up the stairs.

He paused two steps from the top stair. "Where's your suitcase? Do you need anything else from the kitchen? Laundry room?"

Daniel knew the house layout. Which bedroom was hers he might not. Though he probably did. The tall oak he and Kirk used to shinny and sit in outside her bedroom window wasn't anymore. Lightning and a severe windstorm took it out. Would Daniel remember the time he fell through the open window leaning in to kiss her good night? The times he and Kirk kept lookout for each of them? Loving friends. Yes, they'd used the word then. Nothing more than. . .

"Carla, you okay?" Daniel was at the top of the stairs. Deities on high, how long had she been meandering down memory lane caught up in her thoughts? None of them were the same people. Times and experiences had changed them, right?

"I'm great. Tired." She stretched, putting her hand over her mouth hoping Daniel bought the fake yawn. "I think I've got everything from the kitchen. I'll check before we leave. Suitcase is in the middle hall closet."

"I'll get it. You start laying stuff out you want to take with you." Daniel started down the center hall leading away from the landing.

Carla paused where the hall split leading to the back bedrooms and flipped the back hall overhead light on. "Aunt Moriah deeded the house to me. I've made several changes."

Daniel turned back. "It's like a part of us never leave the place we grew up. We carry that with us always."

"This was home for me in many ways. Witchita University is part of me. I found myself there again and again. The short time I called Sylvan Valley home is part of me." Carla pointed to the open bedroom door close to the landing. "My room now. Guest room then. Back bedroom and the oak tree outside it are past. I'm glad I'm here in the present."

"Me too." Daniel squeezed Carla's hand and let go. "I'll grab the suitcase."

He smiled as he opened the closet door. Memories plus experience built the core foundation of who each of them was. Carla's mistrust and uneasiness surfaced some. The next icebreaker might be all of them admitting their trepidations. One thing neither he nor Kirk had done with anyone other than the two of them. Did their mistrust signal failure ahead or a barrier that they needed to tear down together? Speculating wasn't going to solve anything. Getting Carla and him to his place safely did.

CHAPTER EIGHT

Carla entered her bedroom. Grabbing clothes and stuffing them in the suitcase could convey mixed messages. Daniel might think she was in a hurry to get to his place. Part of her was rushing to get through her uneasiness. Face her fears and skip past them wasn't going to solve things either. She paused close to her dresser. She'd packed for a previous trip with Daniel. The trip that led to her parents confronting her outside their home. Confrontation and accusations rang out. Neighbors watched behind curtains until one of them challenged her father about his shouting. Taking the fight indoors hadn't happened. Daniel had escaped by jumping in his car and speeding away. Days later, her family had whisked her away, leaving relatives to pack up the house and their remaining personal effects. Witchery, Nevada, had left a sour taste in her mouth the first year there. As time passed, she made friends and gained covert independence. Friends who covered for her. Taught her easy sleight of hand magic that fooled her parents into thinking she was a late bloomer magical.

"Got the suitcase." Daniel stepped into the room. "You prefer I wait downstairs?"

Carla pulled open the top dresser drawer. "You can put the suitcase on the bed. In the front of my closet are my jeans and long-sleeved tops. Grab three of each, please."

Daniel laid the suitcase on the bed and opened it. "Sure. Are you sure three of each is enough?"

Carla turned, her hands full of bras and underwear. "I'll take my laundry with me. Should be enough. Got my old jeans in there plus some t-shirts. Won't hurt em if paint gets on them."

Daniel nodded and ducked into the closet. Carla placed the undergarments in the suitcase along with a nightgown. She tossed in socks and a pair of slippers as Daniel exited the closet. He held up the hangers. "This what you want?"

"Thank you." Carla reached for the hangers. Her fingers brushed over Daniel's. Heat swirled around and over her fingers, across the tips and trickled on to Daniel. He looked up. His chest slowly rose and fell with each breath he took.

"I'll put them in the suitcase. What else you want out of there?" Daniel pulled his hand away. He pulled the jeans and sweaters off the hangers, dropping the clothes in the suitcase.

"Top of the shoe rack are my sneakers. Those and the long-sleeved denim shirt is it." Carla folded the jeans and sweaters. She quickly tucked her robe into the suitcase. She tossed two novels and her journal in her travel tote.

"Got your sneakers and the shirt." Daniel held up the purple and pink paisley print laundry bag. "Grabbed this, too."

Carla smiled. "Thanks. I've got a few things in the laundry room to put in there."

She wrapped her sneakers in the shirt, put them in the suitcase and closed it. "I'll get the stuff from the laundry room. Will you take the suitcase down? Oh, do I need to bring toiletries?"

"Got shampoo and soap. Nothing fancy," Daniel picked up the suitcase. "Do we need to get your toothbrush, toothpaste and hairbrush before we head downstairs?"

Carla slipped the tote bag over her shoulder and grabbed the laundry bag. "In the downstairs half bath. Use them before I head out to work."

"Half baths come in handy." Daniel chuckled. "First one my parents had was when they got the two-story Clarkson place on the edge of town. My siblings couldn't figure out why the builder forgot to put a tub in the bathroom. They figured it was a half bath cuz no one could wash up in it."

"Aunt Moriah's brother-in-law swore half baths got their name cuz they were half the size of full bathrooms." Carla started down the stairs. "I'll be back in a moment."

Daniel followed Carla down the stairs. He set the suitcase next to the door. His phone buzzed twice. He pulled the phone out of his jacket pocket. Two text messages showed. Both from Kirk. One about delays along Main Street due to overnight road repairs. The second was he arrived safely. Daniel pulled on his jacket as Carla entered the living room.

"Okay, to go." Carla zipped up her jacket. She turned a circle like she was looking for something. Daniel reached for the laundry bag as she faced him. "I got that."

"All right. Everything locked up?" Daniel picked up the suitcase and exited the house. Carla stood in the open door, looked back over her shoulder, and let go a deep sigh. One that she couldn't muffle if she'd wanted to. Had Carla changed her mind?

"I wish I could get a handle on my uneasiness." Carla pulled the front door closed and locked it. "I can't name a reason why."

Daniel took the laundry bag from her. "Perhaps new and old mixing. Your experience around us. Concerning Kirk and I. We've had our moments too."

"Why? You both were always certain I was your chosen one." Carla followed Daniel down the steps.

"Is anyone completely sure? We all have moments. We're not taught to trust ourselves. Value our feelings. Second sight runs in shapeshifters and witches. It can kick your ass." Daniel stood next to his car. "It sure has kicked mine several times."

Carla beeped her car's trunk open. "When did you find out about your ESP abilities?"

Daniel put her suitcase and laundry bag in the car and closed the trunk. "Stumbled on the info after reading a couple of articles researching dream visions. My Great Aunt Susana had them. She left me her journal and family genealogy documents. Weird reading about your ancestors' untold tales and those confirming your family's peculiarities."

Carla smiled. "Yeah, my cousin Nick twice removed isn't magical either. Glad I'm not the only one."

"Science and research can be good or bad depending on your point of view." Daniel unlocked his car. "We're twenty minutes from my place. Kirk texted me he arrived fifteen minutes ago. Are you ready and *sure* about this?"

"Sure as I can be. We've got unfinished things between us. All three of us." Carla opened her car door. "I trust you and Kirk. If I didn't, I wouldn't be here or going with you."

Daniel stepped closer and brushed his lips over hers. "I'm glad. We've each got trepidations. Maybe that is where our discussion needs to continue once we're all together."

"Possibly. Kirk has a say." Carla got in her car. As she reached for the door, she added, "I'm done with letting fear drive. Talking is on once we get to your place. Lead the way."

Daniel nodded. Would Kirk be ready to dive in? How ready was he to take their discussion to a new level? One that included what they each feared, worried would happen, along with concerns. Could their discussion finish the one they started decades ago? Move into the here and now at the same time?

Kirk checked his phone. Daniel's reply to his text and the on their way messages arrived back to back. Daniel's last text puzzled him. *Need to talk when get there. Are you ready to mend and heal at the same time? Move into now?*

Heal and move into now simultaneously. Tricky thing. Letting go and moving forward. Like riding a rollercoaster hoping that your seatbelt and the grab bar kept you from flying out as you topped the large dip and glanced down. Picking up speed pulled you straight out of your seat. Your ass and the seat parted company for a few seconds. It seemed like time stopped until you hit the bottom of the dip and revved up to head to the top of the next dip. Kirk shuddered. He never did like riding roller coasters. Skydiving was too much like roller coaster riding. He wasn't doing either again. His father could fuss all he wanted about paratroopers and the Air Force. One messed up ankle and bruised ass was enough. Military service was not his future nor his end all.

Kirk sat in the patio lounge close to the back door. Stars twinkled into view. Small patches at first. More littering the darkness until the familiar constellations greeted him. Constellations names Cauldron Falls teens came up with. Star maps that guided them unlike the ones their ancestors or government space agencies used. North star was north star like the star gazers of old and current said. South star was south star as well. Night vision and familiarity with the woods and landscape guided them on full moon runs and during the almost pitch-black wild hunts. Being Alpha was like owning his own business. CEO and boss. Partnering with Daniel as co-alpha made sharing Alpha duties a lot easier. There was still a lot to learn and do.

What was his answer to Daniel's text? Heal for sure. Move into now? Did now have a description? A mutual idea that the three of them agreed upon? Were they ready to unite and work as a triad focused on their future? Others were involved. Carla's employees. The packs forming the new joint pack. Maybe the answer was one step at a time. One moment at a time and knowing plans often changed.

Kirk glanced at his phone. Ten minutes had passed. Ten minutes of soul searching. The first he'd done alone since he and Daniel decided to take a leap of faith about Carla. Faith in their connection. Faith it was still strong and real. A belief things could work out. They'd been so close back then. The small amount of time they'd interacted tonight smoked with desire. Blazed with emotions. He bet all their auras sizzled and oozed with reds and yellows. There was no mistaking the passion packed into Carla's kisses. Her self-acceptance came across as strong and centered. Could he and Daniel embrace their inner strengths and be secure in their decision to mutually court Carla? Questions. Some with answers. Some with knowns. Others needed time and research. In the end, they either succeeded or—there was no failure. Their friendship and connection were strong. That much he knew for sure. Kirk pushed his cell phone into his jacket pocket. His answer to Daniel's text wasn't another text. He would answer in person. Face Carla and Daniel and voice his decision aloud. One that he was sure he wouldn't regret as he learned along the way the person each of them were here and now. Not a fantasy one made up of supposition and fear.

Daniel pushed the open button on the garage door opener as he pulled into his drive. Through the garage's back window, he could see the edge of Kirk's truck. Probably had his neighbors guessing who was sneaking into his backyard. Let them guess. The stealth cover of night would keep them guessing. The town gossips' cell phones were buzzing with text or their online chat overloaded with speculation. They didn't know Uncle Zac's steadfast rule was part of the new co-alphas' rules. Steadfast rule said let people talk. Let the gossips speculate. Let those that needed to know know about what affected them. Beyond that, alphas's personal business was that. Personal and not for every pack member or the citizens of Cauldron Falls to know.

Daniel glanced in the rearview mirror. Carla pulled in behind him. He got out of his car and motioned her forward, pointing to the open space on the left side of the garage.

Carla opened her window. "Park there?"

"Yes. I'll pull in next to you. You can see Kirk's truck through the window." Daniel stepped back allowing Carla room to maneuver her car into the garage.

Carla put her car in park, turned the engine off and slowly exhaled. Twice on the way here, fear had roared demanding she listen and act on its demands. Talking her inner scared teen self down off the fear ledge had taken several moments. Moments that four stop lights provided. Aunt Moriah definitely would applaud her courage and assertive self-talk. Fear tossed what-ifs, thin accusations and bits and pieces of rhetoric her parents and extended family members constantly refrained at her as she went from a young teen woman basking in the glow of two men adoring her. Wanting her and finding her beautiful as she was. Accepting her for who she was. Daniel and Kirk were doing the same now. Short time and not a lot of info. Nothing was ever promised to turn out all right all the time. She knew there were some risks involved. When she listened to her heart and psyche, both told her take the moment and enjoy. The outcome didn't demand or need perfection.

CHAPTER NINE

Daniel pulled his car in next to Carla's. He got out, unlocked the door leading into the house and flipped on the mud room interior light. Warm yellow light flowed out into the garage. He stepped back. Carla sat in her car. Why? Uncertainty? Possibly. It probably tagged each of them, tried to touch their hearts and minds in ways that past experiences seized and shouted things had to be that way again. Together, they were stronger. Knew that the past was done, overwith and they'd grown. Changed and learned new ways of being. Daniel pressed his lips together hoping to suppress his smirk. Laughing at his inane thoughts wasn't always easy. It took focus. Focus that needed redirection. Carla needed reassurance.

He reached for the handle of Carla's car door. A click greeted him. Sounds of a door ready to open or was she locking it? Locking herself inside? He reached up prepared to wrap on the window when the door opened partway. The light inside the car showed Carla rummaging in her fanny pack she'd taken off to drive. "Everything okay? Lose something?"

Carla startled, dropped her fanny pack on the passenger seat. She let go of the fanny pack's strap and turned slightly in the driver's seat. "Sorry lost in thought. I put my cell phone in the holder for easy driving access. I tossed it on the seat at the last stop sign. Can't find it."

"No worries. I'll check on that side." Daniel walked around the car and opened the passenger door.

Carla hastily unfastened her seatbelt. Blasted cell phone had slipped out of her hand. She fumbled trying to clasp it. Her palms were sweating. She'd stuttered every time she'd cursed her butterflied-filled stomach clamored for attention. Why had her calm and assurety fled?

"It's okay. I can check. I'll pop the trunk open. You can take my suitcase and laundry bag in." Carla pushed the trunk release.

"No, we're going to find it together." Daniel slid his hand across the passenger seat. "It's either between the seat cushions or on the floor under the seat."

Carla focused on one thing as she made her way around the front of the car. Daniel was helping because he wanted to. He wasn't helping because he didn't think she could do it on her own. The key word was together. Nothing about can't do it by herself. Letting go of the past was part of moving into the present. "The release bar will move the seat back further."

"Thanks. Used to the seat power controls on my car." Daniel moved the seat back. The overhead interior light shined on the floor mat. "Nothing there. Seat recline?"

"Yes, lever on the side. Open the back door and see if there's anything on the floor after I recline the seat." Carla was beside Daniel.

Daniel opened the passenger back door and leaned in. "Not seeing anything yet. Go ahead and recline."

"Watch out. Don't want to hit you with the seat." Carla sat in the seat, pushed the lever back, and reclined until she could see part of Daniel's shoulders.

"Heard something thud." Daniel backed up and out of the back seat area. "Put the seat upright and move it forward as far as you can."

Carla got out, uprighted the seat and moved it forward as far as the seat would go.

"Got it! Teamwork wins!" Daniel retrieved the phone off the backseat floor. "No wonder we couldn't see it. Wedged between the seat cushions at an angle."

"Thank you." Carla put the phone in her jacket pocket. "Won't get out of there too easily."

"You're welcome. Let's get your stuff inside." Daniel got the laundry bag and suitcase out of the trunk.

"Need more help?" Kirk asked, entering the garage.

"Make your choice." Daniel pointed at the laundry bag and suitcase. Kirk set the laundry bag inside and held the door open for Daniel. Both stood in the doorway watching her.

Carla grabbed her fanny pack off the passenger seat, fastened the fanny pack around her waist, closed the passenger doors and made her way back around the car. She patted her pockets checking for her keys. Metal jangles sounded. Keys were where she remembered putting them. She closed the driver's door, fished her keys out, clicked the lock fob and repocketed her keys. She turned, hoping the smile she curled her lips into didn't appear fake. The moment she walked up the steps into Daniel's house, she entered a new dimension of being. A new phase of her life. How much of her past could she dump and not retrieve? How good were any of them at resetting the fulcrum of them as a triadic relationship?

Daniel moved away from the door into his kitchen. Kirk followed him carrying the laundry bag. Daniel turned checking to see if Carla followed. The look on her face as she started up the steps let on to her uneasiness. He'd be the first to admit feeling uneasy and this was his home. His sanctuary. First time Kirk had come over had been unnerving, too. He and Kirk had talked out boundaries and needs that evening over a few beers. They'd fallen asleep lounging on the loveseat and sofa. Sometime after midnight, they'd stumbled into the master bedroom. He fell asleep on his king-size bed and Kirk on the futon in the corner of the master bedroom. Thankful neither of them suffered hangovers the next morning, they laughed at their fears, admitted their friendship was a bromance that no one was going to break.

Carla slowly stepped into the house. She looked behind her and back to him and Kirk. "How do you close your garage door?"

"Button on the wall to the left. Push it and the door closes and shuts off the overhead light."

Kirk stepped forward, holding out his hand. "Would a hug help?"

Carla held up her hand. "Garage door first. Then hugs for each of us."

The clank of the door closing sounded signaling their communal entrance into the new dimension of them and their next phase. Carla pulled her cell phone out of her jacket pocket and put it in her fanny pack's main compartment. As she zipped her fanny pack closed, she moved deeper into the interior of Daniel's home. Not his parents' old house or the familiarity of her place. This was new and different. How different for each of them she didn't know.

Daniel leaned against the doorjamb separating the kitchen from the dining room. Carla's energy signature chilled the air faster than letting in blizzard-cold air. Her hesitation and flat tone spoke volumes. What was going on? Her earlier affect was standoffish with curiosity. She'd kissed Kirk and him like she wanted more. She'd hugged and joked with him as she packed. Had reality smacked her psyche like it had him? Maybe Kirk's, too.

Kirk stood middle of the kitchen, waiting and watching. His barely perceptible shrug spoke almost as loud as Carla's hesitation and flat affect did.

Had they all reverted to the first time they recognized their shared attraction? Back to their teen angst-filled moment? Their first attempt at shared attraction? His and Kirk's bromance acknowledged?

Daniel set Carla's suitcase down. He moved toward Carla as he spoke. "Carla, it's okay."

"Yeah, I know." Carla pulled out a chair from the kitchen table and sat in it. "I've hit the mental I'm tired sputters."

"I remember those." Kirk sat next to Carla. "We've been on high-level energy for the better part of the night."

Daniel sat in the chair across from Carla and Kirk and glanced at his watch. "Praise Lupa, it's almost two in the morning."

"No wonder I feel like I've morphed twice and slept in a hole." Kirk grinned, adding, "First and only time I got shifter drunk. Macken's mash barrel was no place to hide from the Sadie Hawkins full moon she wolfs."

Daniel chuckled. "It took me three days to get the stink out of my clothes much less my parents' car. Most connived bullshit story I ever came up with. The twinkle in my granddad's eyes as I told it said he knew the manure pile was good and deep that night."

Kirk shook his head. "My hangover hung on for two days. Wasn't until I ran into Doc McKinnley and he goaded me into shifting again I sobered up."

"Goaded you?" Carla asked.

"Yup. Doc McKinnley knew doctoring whether it be animal or human or in between. He fed me, told me the facts of shifter biology and gave me some clothes. I didn't need to streak down the back alleys trying to get to the thrift store to grab clothes out of the donation box."

Carla tittered. "Mrs. Griswold kept asking why the donation bags didn't match up with the charity slips given out. My sisters kept saying they didn't know anything."

"Most of us knew the below-the-radar gossip. Rumors ran high and loud. The ones privy to what was going on kept mouths shut." Daniel pushed back from the table. "How about a snack? Then we get some sleep."

"Sounds good." Kirk pointed to the bag on the counter. "Stuff Siobhan sent with us. I put the yogurt in the fridge."

Carla stood. "I'll warm up the croissants."

"Chamomile tea?" Daniel filled the electric kettle and plugged it in. "Got some other herbal tea if you prefer."

Kirk yawned and stretched. "Chamomile helps me sleep. Bit of food, shuck my clothes and I'm ready to sleep."

Carla put three croissants in the microwave to warm. She placed the rest of the food in the fridge. She walked back toward the table pressing her hands on her jeans. She hadn't asked Daniel about his house. Didn't know where she'd be sleeping. Where any of them were sleeping.

Daniel hugged her and pointed toward the cabinets close to the kitchen window. "Mugs are in there. Tea bags in the canister closest to the sink."

Kirk put the sugar bowl on the table along with spoons. "I sense there's an unasked question percolating. I'm gonna answer it."

Oh, you reading minds again?" Daniel filled the mugs, set them on the table and placed a tea bag in each.

"Nope, gave that up after I got too many X-rated minds read." Kirk added sugar to his tea and stirred. "Curious aura color is a pale yellowish green. Some call it the scaredy cat aura."

Carla got the warmed croissants out of the microwave, set them on the table, and sat in her chair. "One thing we promised each other when we first got together was speaking freely. I'm honoring that by asking this. Where are we sleeping tonight?"

Pregnant silence filled the air, growing as they quickly ate and finished their tea. Carla pointed at Daniel and Kirk, repeating her question. "Where are we sleeping tonight?"

Daniel and Kirk glanced at each other and nodded. "With us."

Carla pointed to Kirk and Daniel. "With both of you?"

Daniel nodded. "California King-sized bed. Plenty of room to cuddle, snuggle and a few other things if we're so inclined."

"A few other things?" Carla rose, picking up their dishes.

"AKA sleep." Kirk rose. "Painting duty is for another day."

"I just closed on the house two months ago. Other bedrooms aren't set up. Previous owners had a thing for hideous wallpaper accent walls." Daniel picked up Carla's suitcase. "I don't think any of us could sleep with neon-colored wallpaper glaring at us, even with the lights out."

"Please tell me your bedroom doesn't have this wallpaper." Carla unclenched her hand. She doubted there'd be little sleep unless they reached a mutual agreement. Sex wasn't a forerunner on the other things list.

"No. Pale blues and beige." Daniel moved down the hall, stopping close to an open door.

Carla moved around Daniel and stopped when she blocked the doorway. Her hands on her hips, scowling at Daniel and Kirk. "Did you plan this? Set me up?"

Kirk peered over Daniel's shoulder. "No setup. Hadn't planned on ending up here tonight."

Daniel nodded. "What he said. The most we had in mind tonight was announcing our interest in courting you and talking about it."

Kirk drew a pentagram in the air. "I swear by Lupa and the One. That is all."

CHAPTER TEN

Carla sighed and entered the large master suite bedroom. A wingback chair, ottoman and pole lamp comprised the sitting area in the corner nearest the door. As she turned, her mouth dropped open. On the wall above the dresser was the twelve by eighteen seaside mural they'd drawn and painted together. Daniel had drawn from memory the seaside beach he visited as a child with his grandparents and parents. As more memories returned, they'd added bits and pieces of the seaside city and the tourist attractions. Daniel said those summer trips were some of his fondest childhood memories. Times filled with peace, tranquility and family love.

"I found the mural tucked away in my parents' attic. My sister had tucked it away knowing I'd want it someday. I wish my mom and dad were able to see it." Daniel set her suitcase on the chair.

"One place your parents loved was the shore. Your dad's fascination with aquatic life and preserving the environment drove him to share this with everyone he encountered." Carla ventured further into the room.

"I remember the stories he shared around the scouting campfires. Stories that he often started with a what if and let everyone around the fire add to it." Kirk sat on the futon next to the patio doors on one side of the back wall.

"This room is large enough for us tonight. Are you okay with that?" Daniel entwined his fingers with Carla's.

"Before you answer that." Kirk thumped the futon's cushions. "These aren't the most comfortable to sleep on."

"They might be if you opened the futon up." Daniel turned, pointing toward the alcove area. "Or there's my bed."

Carla walked over to the bed, leaned down and shoved on the mattress with both hands. "No waterbed like you insisted you were going to get for your first place."

Daniel chuckled. "Gave up on that when my cousin showed me his renter's insurance quote. We figured we could drive to Las Vegas, gamble for twenty-four hours and drive back for less."

Kirk rose, yawned and stretched. "I'm voting for sleeping on a comfy mattress. Carla, I promise no naughtiness. I'm too damn tired."

Carla covered her mouth, hoping to stifle her yawn. She lowered her hand and sat on the bed. The plush pillow top mattress cradled her. Calling her to curl up and let the sand mistress cozy her off to dreamland. "Daniel, this is your home and your bed. What's your choice?"

"I've slept ok on the futon. Too tired to deal with folding it out." Daniel yawned. "Kirk, you started something. I'm calling no naked sleeping and everyone in my bed. There's enough room."

Kirk shucked his shirt, tossed it on the bed and headed to the bathroom. "Bag of clothes I brought over still in there?"

"Shelf where you left them. Your toothbrush and paste are on the counter." Daniel sat on the arm of the chair. "Sorry this is impromptu."

"Don't sweat it." Carla got her nightgown and toiletries pack out. "Could have asked questions at my place. Doubt anything could happen if we wanted to. Too dang sleepy."

"True. You use the bathroom next." Daniel yawned again. "Kirk and I can debate who gets which side while you're changing."

Carla smirked. "Debate? None of your famous three-hour discussions and rebuttals."

"Gave those up first year of college." Kirk exited the bathroom wearing faded grey gym shorts. His jeans and briefs flung over his shoulder. "Too many other interesting topics to pursue."

"You did enjoy the eye candy supposedly looking at the night sky through the dorm's telescope." Daniel tossed two small pillows on the futon.

"Never said I didn't. Can't help the Theta-Omega sorority house bedrooms faced toward our dorm." Kirk grabbed his shirt and tossed it with his jeans and briefs on the arm of the wingback chair.

Carla headed toward the bathroom. "Don't let me interrupt your reminiscing."

Kirk waited until the bathroom door clicked shut. He moved closer to Daniel. "Do you think Carla is okay with this?"

"Why do you ask?" Daniel pulled the covers back. "You picking up something I'm not?"

"Nervousness. We're all giving it off some." Kirk plumped the three king-sized pillows on the bed.

"Can't blame her. We announced she is sleeping with us without details." Daniel opened a dresser drawer, rummaged in it, and pulled out a pair of blue sleep shorts. "She could have said no."

Carla cracked open the bathroom door. Kirk and Daniel's voices carried through the room. There was no mistaking what they said. She'd caught part of what they said with the bathroom door closed as they walked by it. She didn't know it took pacing to turn down a bed.

She exited the bathroom, stopping a few steps into the room. Daniel and Kirk faced away from her. The bathroom door hit the wall as she opened it. They were so absorbed in their conversation neither of them registered she was back in the room. Carla walked up behind Daniel. "Or told one of you you were sleeping on the futon."

Kirk jumped to his left, turned around glaring, ready to pounce.

Daniel spun around, his hands waving in the air like he was practicing martial arts moves or getting ready to cast a spell.

Carla walked between Daniel and Kirk. She tossed her clothes in her suitcase and flipped the lid closed. She waited until they both faced her. She blew them a kiss, walked around them, turned and fondled both their asses. "Thanks for the quick thrill, guys. Bedtime. I call dibs on the middle."

Daniel wet one finger, raised it and drew two lines in the air. He drew four more lines in the air as he walked past the bed. He called out, entering the bathroom, "Score. Carla two. Kirk and I zip. Extra points for catching us off guard."

"What Daniel said." Kirk stretched out beside Carla. "You heard the question. What's your answer?"

"Am I nervous?" Carla pulled the sheet up to her waist. "Who wouldn't be?"

Kirk rolled on his side. "Got a point. We've gotten further tonight than ever before."

"I'll second that," Daniel offered, exiting the bathroom. "By the way, I put towels out for us. We can contemplate saving water in the morning. Shower is big enough. We might fit all of us in."

Carla exhaled. Her mind wanted to run rampant with buts, ors and nors concerning the conversation. Her psyche clapped its hand over her mind's rambling mouth and told it to shut up and go to sleep. That was exactly what she was doing. She kissed Kirk. Rolled to Daniel and kissed him. "Conversation for another part of the day. Good night gents."

Daniel glanced at Kirk. Kirk shrugged, pulling the blanket and sheet up over him. Daniel settled the blanket and sheet over him and Carla. He turned off the light. As darkness filled the room, he closed his eyes wondering if they were finally making headway into their reunion phase.

Carla nudged Daniel with her elbow. "Change places."

Daniel blinked and squinted his eyes open. "Huh?"

"Bathroom calls." Carla tossed the covers off them and started scooting down the mattress. "Be right back."

Daniel rolled to the edge of the bed, sat up and held his hand back to her. "Faster this way."

Carla scooted past Daniel and trotted into the bathroom. The clock on the nightstand showed eight-fifteen. They'd gone to sleep around two. Six hours. Six hours sleeping between the two men she trusted more than most. Trust didn't come easy. Some won it with their actions. Others with their words. Those that backed up their actions with words got into her inner circle. Daniel and Kirk were there. Probably never left it. Moving forward meant being vulnerable. Open and honest. Honest with herself and honest in speaking her truth. Carla washed and dried her hands. Moments like these were scary. Scary because her inner self was quiet. Sometimes too bloody quiet. Another hour or two of sleep would help. Self-reflections during morning potty time wasn't something she'd recommend to anyone. Who the hell was awake enough to make sense out of half-awake ramblings?

Kirk rolled over, reached out and—"Why am I touching you?"

Daniel roused and turned partway over, scowling. "What you want?"

"You let her sneak away." Kirk tossed the covers off and sat up.

"Who? What?" Daniel rubbed his eyes. He shoved the covers off him.

"Carla who. What you let her sneak out." Kirk moved to the edge of the bed and stood.

" No he didn't." Carla halted halfway back to the bed.

"Huh?" Kirk turned around. "You're still here."

"Never left unless going to the bathroom is leaving." Carla pointed to the bed. "Maybe you need more sleep."

"I sure the hell do." Daniel held up the blanket and sheet. "Any takers?"

Carla stood on the foot of the bed, walked up between Daniel and Kirk's side of the bed, and dropped on the mattress. She bounced. Carla laughed and grabbed part of the covers. "I'm going back to sleep. My spot's still warm. Kirk, yours might be if you kick your mad out of the way."

Kirk lay down close to her, patted her cheek, pulled the covers back over him and muttered, "Sorry all."

Carla smirked, snuggling down under the blankets, enjoying Kirk and Daniel's warmth. She'd tell Kirk later she accepted his apology. Would Daniel remember? If he did, his acceptance was up to him. She closed her eyes, matched her breathing to Kirk's and Daniels, and dozed off.

Daniel sat up, stretched and glanced at the nightstand clock. Ten-thirty A.M. He'd gotten almost eight hours uninterrupted deep sleep. Kirk's short-burst accusation hadn't roused him that much. His apologetic tone sounded sincere enough. Carla hadn't let it bother her either. Watching her walk across the bed and drop down hard enough to bounce them was worth his mental replay. Daniel grinned as he stood. Carla wasn't taking crap from either of them. Her actions backed that up for sure.

Carla squeezed his hand, turned over and snuggled closer to Kirk. She kissed his cheek.

"Huh? Who?" Kirk turned partially toward Carla. Daniel grinned. Who was half-asleep now?

"Me," Carla whispered. She grabbed part of the covers and billowed them in the air. She stood up, walked to the foot of the bed, turned and announced in a louder voice. "I think you know who now, Kirk."

Daniel pressed his lips together. Mirth pressed against the back of his throat, ready to escape. Carla wasn't letting Kirk off too easily. Daniel wasn't sticking around for the outcome. His bladder decried its priority. He hoped there wasn't any cleanup needed when he got back.

Kirk slowly inhaled, pressing his fingers against the mattress. His wolf grinned in the back of his mind. Laughter echoed through his subconscious. His psyche was probably rolling on the floor laughing its non-existent ass off. The top kicker was he had a hard-on that refused to give up. Damn wet dreams about vivid threesomes. Kirk doubted his were going to come true any time soon.

Daniel re-clicked the bathroom door shut. He grabbed the hand towel and covered his face and mouth with it. Laughter slipped out. He tried lowering the towel. Images of Kirk gawking at Carla and her standing on the end of the bed with her arms folded. . . more laughter erupted. Carla wasn't taking prisoners very easily. She had swooped in and pounced. Daniel splashed his face, dried it and worked to regain his composure. It could be his turn next. Did he take the towel with him for self-defense?

CHAPTER ELEVEN

Daniel cracked the bathroom door open and asked, "Is it safe to come out?"

"Depends on your version of safe." Carla sounded like she was right next to the door.

Crap, how had his turn come? What happened to innocent and non-participating party?

"Safe as in you backing away from the door and giving me room." Daniel opened the door a bit more.

"Get on out here," Kirk called out. "Some of us need a refuge break."

"More like he's got a hardon that needs one of two things. I'm guessing taking a leak tops his list." Carla sounded like she'd moved back from the door some.

"Damn Carla, must you announce it like we need to tell the neighbors?" Kirk trotted toward the bathroom.

"No. If Daniel insists on hiding in the bathroom, want to be sure he understands why you are stampeding his way." Carla opened her suitcase. "My turn next. Shower and dress."

Daniel exited the bathroom, holding the towel behind him. "Shower and dress?"

"Yeah. Time to get on with the day." Carla tossed her jeans and top on the bed. "Get a schedule going."

Daniel shook his head, pulling the towel tight between his hands. "First, none of us need checklists. Second, who appointed you boss lady?"

Carla grinned and pointed at herself. "I did."

Kirk entered the bathroom and called out. "Sounds like a divide and conqueror session happening."

"Divide and conqueror?" Carla faced Daniel as Kirk exited the bathroom.

"Yup. Like when we played Spin-the-Bottle." Kirk closed the space between him and Daniel. "Decided who led and who followed."

Daniel nodded. "Seems like that's happening again."

Carla retreated. Daniel and Kirk moved forward. Kirk two steps to the right. Daniel two steps to the left. Carla bumped up against the futon. She quickly glanced behind her. She grabbed the first thing she put her hand on and pulled it to her.

"Ha! *I'm armed.*" She held the small pillow in front of her.

Daniel flung his arm forward. The small towel in his hand. "I'm armed, too."

Kirk sidestepped quickly toward the bed, reaching for a pillow. "I'm arming."

Daniel moved closer to Carla. "Pulling out the big guns, Kirk?"

"You and Carla ganging up on me?" Kirk gripped the pillow with two hands.

"Defending." Carla inched toward the bed. Kirk swung his pillow back.

Daniel dropped the towel. Grabbed his shorts and tugged them off. "Got a better idea. First one buckass naked in the shower don't gotta cook breakfast."

Carla did an about-face, dropping her pillow on the bed. She snatched part of her nightgown with both hands, pulling it up. "Second naked person in the shower doesn't have to do dishes."

Daniel trotted toward the bathroom. "Only my bathroom shower works. Plumber coming next week to change out the fixtures in the hall bathroom."

Carla tugged her nightgown off, tossing it at Kirk as she looped around him, following Daniel toward the bathroom. She shoved her panties down as she went. "Third naked person in the shower has to wash the first person's back and do dishes."

Kirk tossed the pillow on the bed. Picked up Daniel's shorts, Carla's nightgown and panties. Tossed them on the bed and shucked his shorts. Shower would be full. Very full. Good thing Daniel had gone with the half-glass enclosed walk-in shower. Fitting three would work easier.

Daniel glanced over his shoulder. Carla was right behind him. He entered the shower, turned the handle all the way to hot, stepped back and pointed to the soap bar on the sink. "We'll need it. Kirk is probably right behind us."

Carla clutched the soap. She was nude. Nude with Daniel and Kirk. Something they'd laughed and talked about as teens. Unsure of their bodies and yet curious what the other sex looked like. Supernatural puberty did mimic human. Natural duality, magic or shapeshifter mixed with human left open two puberty trends. Curiosity mixed with pheromonal angst or pheromonal angst plus supernatural genome manifestations. Ah well, she was past both. Latent magic had its blips like menstruation. Praise the One, Aunt Moriah had gotten her past insecurities and inferior feelings. Carla entered the shower. She was comfortable in her own skin and secure with who and where she was in life.

"Room enough for the three of us?" Carla stuck her hand under the shower spray as Daniel adjusted the temperature.

"Crowded." Daniel ducked under the shower spray. "One person having to maneuver past the others as we soap and rinse."

"Chaperone on duty," Kirk called, entering the bathroom. "You two behaving?"

"Oh yeah. Behaving real good." Daniel flicked water at Kirk as he entered the shower enclosure. "What you chaperoning?"

"You show me and then I'll know." Kirk picked up the soap bar off the shower soap dish. He rolled the soap between his hands, working up a lather. "Who needs help soaping up?"

Carla pointed to Daniel. "Daniel's wet. Probably could use the help."

"Not on this chaperone's do list." Kirk swiped one soapy hand down Carla's arm closest to him. "Soaping you, my dear is."

"I think you need this." Carla moved closer to Daniel, holding out her soap bar. "I need more water right now."

"This is like a car wash. One person wet. Soap 'em good and rinse." Daniel ducked his head under the shower spray. He let Carla around him. "Kirk, shampoo, please?'

"Thanks." Carla stepped under the spray. Raised her arms, turning left then right, wetting all of her plus her hair and face.

"Here's chaperone's deal." Kirk pointed at the spray. "Carla gets to wash each of us. Front and back with our help. We get to wash Carla front and back together."

"That's teaming up." Carla looked around Daniel, "What's fair about that?"

"We're touching you. You're touching us." Kirk poured shampoo into Daniel's hand. "Fondling permitted. Chaperone's approval."

"I'm getting washed twice?" Carla tried to move around Daniel.

"I wash one side. Kirk the other." Daniel worked the shampoo through his hair. "Help me rinse my hair. You get a head start on my back and ass."

"You rinse your hair while I shampoo mine." Carla stuck her hand around Daniel. "Kirk, a bit more shampoo, please."

Kirk put a dab of shampoo in Carla's hand. "All set. Carla, you good with doing Daniel first?"

Carla quickly washed and rinsed her hair. She picked up the soap close to her, lathered her hands and set the soap down. "Daniel, your wash down starts now."

Daniel raised his arms. "Wash away, hon."

Carla slicked her soapy hands up and down Daniel's back. Back and forth, reaching partway around his waist. She trailed her fingers through the outer edge of Daniel's pubic hair and back across his ass. She patted both ass cheeks, gave them a five-count squeeze, and pulled her hands away. "Let me past you. I'm water-logged enough."

"Back half done. Front awaiting its turn." Daniel turned sideways. Carla gingerly moved around Daniel, holding onto his arm.

Carla clutched the soap. They'd seen each other naked as teens. Nude as adults was upping the ante. Sexual overtones were no longer teen angst-filled pheromones and hormones popcorning with each touch, kiss and embrace. They'd shucked their clothes on a dare and put them back on quite rapidly after ogling each other for several moments. She worked the soap between her hands, working up a second lather, and laid the soap down. Daniel moved toward her until his hands rested on her shoulders. This was no game of chicken. It was real and about to get absolutely hot and more touchy-feely than she and Daniel had ever been before.

"Carla, take it as slow as you need." Daniel leaned down, brushed his lips over hers and pulled back.

Carla stretched her hands out in front of her laying them on Daniel's waist. If she soaped lower, his pubic hair would caress her palms. Higher and his chest and nipples would pulsate their warmth across her palms, up her arms and cascade deep into her, pooling within her close to her mons. She slid one hand up. The other down. Repeating the motion in opposite directions. She worked her soapy hands over Daniel's shoulders, slowly lowering them until pubic hair tickled her fingertips. She looked up.

Daniel's eyes were closed. His mouth open like he pulled in air. She felt every swell of his chest with each inhale and exhale. She was getting to him.

Carla trailed her fingers through Daniel's pubic hair, working soap into the tight nest of curls. Circles large and small until she touched a part of him she'd seen but never handled.

"*Yes!*" Daniel groaned. "I've dreamed of this. Wanted this and didn't realize how much I needed you to touch me until now."

He rocked back on his heels, clenched his hands, willing his libido to be patient. Carla's hands brushed over his glans and encircled his cock with both hands. Slow slides up and down from the base of him and over the tip of him. Back down again and one hand slicked its way to his groin and cupped his balls. Bathing them with the warmth of her palm. Part of Carla's essence soaked into him and jagged its way deeper into him. He wasn't sure how much more he could withstand. Orgasming could make or break the mood. The flow that was happening. Enveloping all of them.

"I'm going to come if you keep it up." Daniel clasped Carla's wrist. "Enough for now?"

Carla nodded and let go of Daniel. "Another level of newness reached."

"Yeah." Daniel kissed Carla's cheek, turned and quickly rinsed off. "Kirk, your turn."

Kirk glanced behind him. Chilled bench seat tentatively reached toward him with its chilled tendrils aimed for his ass. Not goosing him again! Kirk exited the shower, staying on the bathmat ensuring none of them didn't slip on wet cold tiles. "Carla moves back toward the bench. Daniel and I can trade places."

Carla moved close to the bench. "Chilly."

"Not for long, sweetie." Daniel stepped up on the bench. "Kirk, come on in. The water's great."

Kirk laughed, re-entering the shower. He stuck his hand under the spray. "I wondered if you two were going to use up all the hot water."

"Figured dual large capacity tanks and solar powered would keep water plenty hot." Daniel pointed at the bench as he stepped off it. "Next upgrade is a heated bench. Damn, that is chilly."

Kirk ducked under the spray, combing his hands through his hair. "Shampoo, please."

Carla picked up the bottle. She willed herself to not gawk Kirk. He was ogle-worthy. She'd gotten an eyeful of Daniel during their teen strip and bare-it.

Kirk was the last one to shuck and bare it all. By the time, she'd turned back for a second look, he'd started pulling his clothes on. Now he stood deliciously nude in front of her.

Ginger-colored hair adorned his chest in an inverted V that flowed down to his pubis. Kirk wasn't hiding. His gaze met hers. He held out his hand. Carla licked her lips and moved forward. She blinked as she got closer to Kirk. Flashes of yellow, orange and pale greens erupted at the outer edges of her view. Kirk nodded, motioning her tighter. He leaned down and whispered, "Enjoy the view, darlin'. You're welcome to look all you want."

Carla squeezed shampoo into Kirk's hand, handed Daniel the bottle, and picked up the soap. "Regal. Reminds me of the first nude male photo I saw. Groin was hidden. I wanted to know if his pubic hair matched the hair on his head."

Kirk lathered his hair. "Always has. Naturally matched. Glad you're enjoying the view."

"Touching and washing is my preferred doing." Carla grasped the soap, thrust her hands under the water, and slid both hands down Kirk's chest. Not stopping when she reached his cock. Working the soap gently over his balls and back up his cock once wasn't enough. Palming Kirk's balls, she squeezed and let go.

Kirk grunted and jerked. "Easy darlin'. I'm not into pain. Especially my own."

"Sorry." Carla leaned down and kissed Kirk's cockhead. "Kiss and make better."

Kirk jerked again. "Oh, yeah. Nice. Can't stand much more unless you want a mouth full of me."

Carla lathered her hands again, set the soap down and finished washing Kirk's chest, arms and face. "Turn around while you're rinsing, I'll get your back and cute ass."

Kirk grinned, brushed his lips over hers and turned. He bent over, swinging his ass to and fro as he rinsed his hair and face. "Not tempting you. Letting you get a good start on my ass."

Carla slipped her hand between Kirk's legs, fondling him briefly, slipping and sliding her hands over his ass and lower back. "Guess you want the rest of your back washed too."

"Sure do." Kirk handed her the soap. "Get it done cuz you're next."

Carla soaped Kirk's back as far up as she could. She tapped Kirk's arm. "Got as far as I could. You want Daniel to get the rest?"

"NO!" Daniel and Kirk answered almost simultaneously.

Kirk straightened, turned and rinsed his back. "Guys got limits on touching each other. Mine is my back."

Daniel slipped his arm around Carla's waist. "First time I met Kirk, he wore a shoulder brace. Trigger spot dislocating his shoulder trying to be a super athlete."

"Some days, it likes to remind me." Kirk rubbed his shoulder. "Today is one of them."

"I'm sorry Kirk." Carla reached toward Kirk.

"It's okay." Kirk slid his hand up Carla's arm. He cupped her cheek. "No harm. No foul."

"You get the side closest to you. I got this side." Daniel hugged Carla to him and handed Kirk the soap. Daniel picked up the other bar, soaped his hands and laid them on Carla's shoulder above her breast.

Daniel watched as Carla glanced from Kirk to him. Her lips pressed tight against each other. Kirk lathered his hands, laid the soap in the soap dish and placed his hands below Carla's other breast.

"Wash together at the same time or separately? Carla, your choice." Kirk nipped her neck. Captured her earlobe between his teeth, worried and suckled it, and let go.

CHAPTER TWELVE

Carla slowly exhaled, relaxing into Kirk and Daniel's joint embrace. They'd shared hugs before. Hugs that left them wanting more, needing more and unable to do more. This time more was proceeding. "One of the things I promised my virginal self was trusting you two with my first time. Both of you deflowering me in different ways. None of us are virgins."

"No. Something important to us then. Is important now, too." Daniel kissed her cheek. "Consent. We're here because we want to be."

"I'm here because I want to be." Carla put her palms on Daniel and Kirk. "Wash me, please."

Kirk worked his soapy hands over and under her breast. His thumb flicked across her nipple, slowly stroking circles around its base and down close to her mons. He stopped at the top of her thigh, close to the apex of her legs. Daniel copied Kirk's moves. Their hands rested close to her labia. Either could reach in and stroke her clit.

"I'm going to stroke your clit a bit. Watch you have a mini orgasm for me." Kirk slid two fingers between her labia lips. He worked his fingers back and forth until he caught her pleasurable spot close to the top of her clitoris. Slow strokes followed by bits of pressure.

Carla grasped Kirk's arm. "I'm wet. Close to a bigger orgasm."

Kirk kissed her cheek and slowly withdrew his fingers.

Daniel leaned down, capturing the nipple of her breast closest to him. He suckled and worried the nipple with his lips and tongue. Carla gripped Daniel's arm, still holding on to Kirk. Who'd taught Daniel about nipple orgasms? The pounding vibrations that sparked and sizzled their way straight to her clit and g spot. Much more and...

"*Yes-s-s,*" Carla moaned. "Much more, and I'm gonna need a nap."

Daniel let go of her nipple, kissed her lips and slid past her. "Rinsing is our best option. Either that or we're gonna have to hunt down the condoms."

Carla ducked under the spray, sluicing the water and soap off her. She cupped water in both hands, rinsed her mons and labia twice and exited the shower. Kirk rinsed next and exited. Daniel rinsed, turned the shower off and took the towel Carla held out. Taking turns drying backs, they dried off in between kisses and touches.

Kirk and Carla dressed quickly. Kirk muttered about food and coffee as he pulled his shorts on. Carla teased him about being a coffee snob when he asked Daniel twice about what flavored coffee did he have in stock. Daniel hung the damp towels up, tossed the bathmat over the top of the shower divider and opened the mirror cabinet over the sink. He checked the date on the box. Expiration date was two months hence. He set the box of condoms on the nightstand. Glad he'd listen to his second sight. It was the first time in a long time it pointed him in the right direction.

Daniel chuckled as he made his way to the kitchen. Carla was opening and closing cabinets looking for the coffee maker. Kirk asked who was cooking. He reminded Carla he burned the last batch of pancakes he tried to make. Daniel entered the kitchen hoping he didn't need to assign kitchen duties.

"Daniel, you've got quiche ingredients in here." Carla closed the fridge door. "It'll take forty minutes to prep and bake."

"What kind of quiche?" Kirk filled the coffee maker with water and amaretto-flavored coffee.

"Eggs, cheddar jack cheese, and sausage." Carla put three mugs out next to the coffee maker. "French bread toasted with jam and butter. I saw the jam jar behind the carton of half and half."

Daniel laid the morning newspaper on the table. "Sounds good. I'll put a delivery order in with the market later on."

"We didn't grill the steaks I brought over. How about those with baked potatoes smothered with butter and sour cream?" Kirk rubbed his growling stomach.

"Breakfast first." Carla pointed to the coffee maker. "It works better if you turn it on."

Kirk sheepishly grinned and clicked the on button. "Need food and caffeine."

"Three hands prepping food gets it ready quicker and easier." Daniel sprayed a baking pan with olive oil.

"Kirk, you're in charge of chopping up the sausage." Daniel put three patties on the cutting board and held out a meat cleaver. "Chopping sausage. Nothing else okay?"

"Somehow, there's a story behind that." Carla set the egg carton on the counter next to the bowl Daniel put out.

"There is." Daniel glanced at Kirk.

"I'm telling it. It's my story." Kirk held up the meat cleaver. "Shifter scouting camp expedition. Scout leader was in charge of packing equipment. Had checklist. Checked it twice."

Daniel snickered. "Yeah, Uncle Max, the great teacher. Not so great practical person."

"Is this the Uncle Max who swore up and down he could lead this scouting thing with his eyes closed and half-shifted?" Carla cracked six eggs into the bowl, tossed the shells in the sink disposal and put the carton back in the fridge.

"Yup." Daniel set the half-and-half next to the egg bowl. "Kirk and I suggested he check the list thrice."

"What do you mean check it thrice?" Kirk asked in a mimicked deep voice. "Uncle Max never spoke softly. The entire PTA gathering heard him from two schoolroom doors down the hall."

"The entire troop acquiesced. We loaded up the gear reassured we had everything we needed." Daniel turned on the oven to preheat. "Tents, sleeping bags, coolers, grill grate, and two huge trash bags with tags that read miscellaneous."

"Sausage done. How about a hashbrown crust as the basis?" Kirk rinsed off the meat cleaver. "Darkness hits, wind is blowing. Seven hungry wolf cub shifters, two bear ones and one male witch are pacing like they ain't eaten for months instead of a few hours."

"Grate away." Daniel set out the grater and two potatoes. "Uncle Max tells Kirk and I to get the axe and chop some wood for the cooking fire."

"Two huge bags dumped. Sleeping bags, tents and coolers gone through." Kirk brandishes the meat cleaver. "Makes a handy wood chopper. Especially when there are four of them packed."

Carla clasped the half-and-half carton with both hands, carefully set it on the counter, walked over to the table, pulled out a chair and dropped into it laughing. She held her sides, laughing louder and more each time she looked at Kirk and Daniel both standing there nodding and grinning. She wiped tears off her cheeks. "Did Uncle Max lead any other expeditions?"

"Uncle Max retired from Scout Leadership very quickly." Daniel washed and dried the meat cleaver. "Rumor is his wife threatened to chop off his tail next full moon morph with not one but all three of her dulled meat cleavers if he didn't step down."

"Uncle Max hightailed it out of town taking his intact tail and self with him. Aunt Hattie happily signed divorce papers a few months later." Kirk poured coffee into the three mugs and placed them on the table. "Aunt Hattie ran the best bakery in Cauldron Falls. Her diced ham and cheese croissants sold out every time she made them. She gifted the recipe to Siobhan's chef and buried the ruined meat cleavers with a full funeral service."

"OMG!" Carla clapped her hand over her mouth trying to keep her peels of laughter in check. "That is what the marker at the base of the founders' rock is about?"

"You got it. Here they lie. They gave their all. Their saga don't ask cuz they won't tell." Daniel added half and half to the eggs, whisked them and added the shredded cheddar jack cheese and sausage. "Potatoes ready?"

Kirk lined the baking pan with the hash browns. "Fill it up. And bake."

Daniel poured the egg mixture onto the hash browns, tapped the pan some to even the mixture out and cover all the hash browns. He placed it in the oven, set the timer for forty minutes and ran water in the bowl.

Kirk sat in the chair next to Carla. "This morning's play in the shower tells me one thing."

Daniel sat across from Carla and Kirk. "I'm probably thinking the same thing. You share first."

Kirk sipped his coffee and set his mug down. "We're still attracted to each other. We've got chemistry happening. Like it simmered below and boiled back up to the surface once we got close enough."

"Can't deny what happened." Carla added two sugar cubes to her coffee plus a smidgen of half and half. "Daniel, your thoughts, please."

"Run parallel to Kirk's. You're right, Carla there's no denying what's happening." Daniel stirred his coffee and sipped. He set the mug down and asked, "Are you saying you aren't attracted?"

Carla rubbed her mug with her hands. Topic wasn't about what was. It was about here and now. Present company and feelings. Chemistry was definitely happening. Catalytic effects happening like they waited until their dormant period ended. Or was it nudged them into full-blown aliveness? She looked up. Daniel and Kirk watched her. Some would say they watch their prey ready to pounce. She read the look differently. Their eyes mirrored their concerns. Neither glared or scowled. "I'm attracted. Wouldn't be here if I wasn't, wouldn't have kissed you both like I did, and I stepped into this with eyes and heart open. Conscience might be tapping me here and there. Past experience doesn't always shut up."

"Thanks." Kirk laid his hand next to Carla's. "What's next? Where do we go from here?'

Daniel checked the oven timer. "Twenty-five more minutes. Do we want more? More than now? Something long-term?"

Carla drank several swallows of coffee. "I've changed. You've each changed. We've got a foundation started. It's got chunks missing. Lots of brick and mortar like one of my customers says. Solid building comes with a secure and strong foundation."

"We've hit some hurdles full throttle. Others stumbled around them or over them. Maybe both." Kirk started to move his hand away. Carla laid her hand on his, squeezed it and let go.

"I think we each need to bring each other into the current by introducing who we are now. Possibly the high points of what got us here." Daniel set plates, utensils and napkins on the table. "Who's toasting the French bread?"

Carla stood. "I am. Trick a French foreign exchange witch shared with me. I use it for Maxson's Brunch Toast Menu item."

"I'll go first with my reintroduction." Kirk turned in his chair enabling him to see Daniel and Carla easier. "Hi, I'm Kirk. My day job morphed into head accountant for a firm that folded during Covid. Not enough business to sustain keeping five hundred employees. I fell in love with balance sheets and ledgers taking an accounting class in college. When I'm not busy balancing monthly bills and accounts for contracted businesses and clients, I'm one of Cauldron Falls' new co-alphas."

"Hi Kirk." Carla waved and went back to slicing the half loaf of French bread into toastable slices. "I expected something different. It's what we would do at the reunion if we attended it."

Daniel set a wolf-shaped trivet on the table. "I'm next. Hi, I'm Daniel. One of Cauldron Falls's male witches. Local business entreprenuer. After making my fortune buying and selling exotic antique cars and large venture investments, I decided to take up funding local start-up businesses."

Carla buttered several slices of French bread, laid them butter side down in the skillet, and turned the burner to simmer. She rinsed her hands and sat in her chair. "Here's mine. I'm Carla. Maxson's newest owner. My magic is cooking, organization, and an innate business acumen. A few friends call it intuition. Others extra sensory perception."

Timer buzzed. Daniel took the quiche out of the oven and set it on the trivet center of the table. "I left out I'm co-alpha with Kirk. New pack blending. New hybrid packs forming. Exciting times and cautious ones, too. Before we eat, how about an interesting fact or two more about us."

"Trigger the conversation better than we did last night ." Kirk chuckled. "My interesting two facts are I've got a bum ankle same side as my bum shoulder. I shapeshift at will. No full moon needed."

Daniel laid a sharp knife on the table. "Carla, toast almost done?"

"Yes. Just need jam jar from the fridge." Carla set the plate of toasted French bread on the table next to the quiche pan. "My two interesting facts are I escaped Witchery, Nevada and I ran away from home to do it."

Daniel set the jam jar and spoon next to the quiche. "Aunt Naomi's blueberry compote jam straight from her blueberry bushes and kitchen."

Kirk gleefully rubbed his hands together. "One spoonful is never enough."

"Yeah, not eating the whole jar is enough. Save some for Carla and me." Daniel refilled their mugs and sat down. He passed a plate with two quiche pieces to Kirk.

Kirk put two pieces of toast on the plate next to the quiche, saluted them with his fork and began eating.

Carla grinned. Kirk enjoyed good food as much as he did his coffee and friends. She put two quiche pieces and two pieces of toast on a plate. "Here you go, Daniel."

"Thank you." Daniel set his plate in front of him and dug in.

Carla put the last two quiche pieces on her plate, pulled the jam jar to her, and snatched three toast pieces off the toast plate. Kirk pointed his fork at her, shaking his head. She nodded and opened the jam jar. Took the spoon and put a large dollop of jam on each of her toast pieces.

CHAPTER THIRTEEN

They ate in companionable silence for several moments. Kirk set the jam jar center of the table as he spoke. "What is long-term for us?"

Daniel took the jam jar from Kirk, slattered jam on the last piece of toast and laid it on his plate. "I don't think we can set a time frame. Courting each other is something we all want. What is courting? What do we want from it?"

"We came close to friends with benefits at one point. Our shower play showed we're open to that. I guess we're talking about more than friends." Carla finished her toast and the last of her coffee.

" Agreed. I believe we've got a second chance. A second chance to go for what we want." Kirk wiped his mouth and tossed his napkin on his empty plate.

Daniel ate the last of his toast and wiped his hands with his napkin. "Carla, you're the centerpiece. What are your thoughts?"

"I've thought about each of you over the years. What if either of you came back into my life. I hadn't given much thought to what if you both did. It's an interesting aspect." Carla put her dishes in the sink. "I think we need to know more about our inner cores individually before we jump into yes we're a family threesome."

Kirk pushed back from the table. "How about each of us tells our tale like we're catching each other up?"

Daniel added his and Kirk's dishes to the others in the sink. "Carla and I've got laundry. Kirk, I bet you got laundry, too."

Carla sighed. "The never-ending saga of life chores and fitting them in."

"Conversation helps them go faster." Daniel squirted dish detergent on the dishes, filled the sink with hot water, and held out the towel and dish sponge. "Who's washing? Drying? Sorting laundry?"

Kirk grabbed the dish sponge. "I'll wash. Clean up the counters and stove."

Daniel tossed the towel over his shoulder. "Guess that leaves me drying. Carla, do you mind sorting laundry?"

"Sorting, okay. Laundry is everyone's responsibility." Carla pushed her laundry bag to the table, set Daniel's laundry basket on the table, and started toward the laundry room. "Everything better be down here. I'm not scavenger hunting dirty duds."

Kirk thrust his hands into the soapy water. Swirled his hands and sponge through the sink twice and started washing a mug. "My mother tried to make chores a game. Go hunt down something like trash or laundry. Except my siblings never put their stuff in usual places."

Daniel ran rinse water in the second of the double sinks. "Being the youngest meant you got the chores the older ones didn't want or didn't do. To this day I can scrub a floor and wax floors that rival restaurant cleaning standards. Or clean up messes quicker than most. Why? I learned human ways of doing it."

Carla set two baskets on the floor next to the table and sat down. "Tsk, Tsk both of you. I'm the only one out of seven siblings who can keep house, cook, and run a business without magic or supernatural intervention."

"Got dumped on good by your family." Daniel rinsed and dried two mugs.

"Disrespected and mistreated is what it was." Carla tossed several pieces of clothing in a basket. "In their minds, I was never good enough. Always had to try harder. Stop being lazy doing things non-magically."

Kirk placed the last of their breakfast dishes in the rinse water. He held up the sponge. "My military father pushed my brothers and me harder than he did our sisters. Us boys had to keep house, cook, clean and do laundry. Sisters were princesses. Princess pains in the ass!"

"I overheard one talk your dad gave your youngest sister about going for the prime shapeshifter male in her class." Daniel finished drying the dishes and emptied the rinse water. "He said gotta get the cream of the crop. Remember, your mom and I are counting on you taking care of us in our old age."

"We laughed out of earshot quite a bit." Kirk wiped down the counter and stove. He rinsed out the sponge, wrung it out, and laid it in the soap dish on the window sill. "Both my sisters married outside the pack. One is divorced. The other told my dad to piss up a rope and don't darken her doorstep until he could accept her marriage and his grandkids."

Carla held up two pairs of paisley print briefs. "I don't care who's these are. How new are they? Don't need colors bleeding."

Daniel tossed the damp dish towel in the basket of light-colored clothes. "I'll get you another basket. Cold water wash and rinse. Got a few things like that."

Carla grabbed Daniel's arm. "It's all cold water wash and rinse. Saves on energy, environmental impact, and don't need worry about bleach spots. Non-chlorine bleach if needed."

Daniel pointed at the basket with light-colored clothes in it. "Had 'em a while. Color catcher cloths are next to the washer. Add to each load for safety."

Carla opened and set her laundry bag on the floor. "Kirk, your dad was a royal pita at times. Royal pain in the ass. So were my parents. Leaving Witchery was a good thing. It wasn't ultra bad the time I was there."

Kirk sat in the chair next to Carla. "Do you mind sharing details? I'd like to know more. "

Carla rose walked to the counter and turned. "Depends. I'd like to know more about your and Daniel's time away. How do you feel about sharing details and more?"

Daniel set two baskets of strawberries and blueberries on the counter. "I don't mind talking and doing. It keeps the subconscious distracted. How about a group lunch and dinner prep while we reminisce?"

Kirk picked up one of the baskets. "I'm good with doing and talking. Similar move scored my ex-wife."

Carla picked up the second basket. "Scored you a wife? Is that how you see this?"

Kirk dropped the basket, strode to Carla, and stopped when he was beside her. "One, Diana and I never planned to marry. We got suckered into it. Two, you aren't being scored or suckered into anything. Daniel and I talked and agreed on courting you. You say you're here and on board 'cuz you want to be. Right?"

Daniel stuck his arm between Carla and Kirk. "Turn and take two steps away from each other. Cooler heads prevail for all of us, please."

Kirk turned, took two steps and faced Daniel and Carla. "Apology to you both. Trigger response."

Carla sighed and sat down. "This is what I feared. Now I'm decompressing. I don't have to be on the defensive. I've spent so long guarding my heart and self, I'm trigger-ready to jump and fuss."

Daniel filled glasses with ice, lemon slices and water and set them on the table. "We've each got triggers. Let's get them out. Hear each out and help the healing continue."

Carla drank a third of her water. "Part of my moodiness is too much coffee. I usually have three cups spread throughout the day. Not back to back. Sugar rush, too."

"Probably true for each. Systems grabbing sugar, food, and caffeine all at once." Kirk sat, drank water and set the glass down. "Since I inadvertently started the catch-up conversation, I'll continue, okay?"

Carla and Daniel nodded.

Kirk shrugged and continued telling his tale. "Diana and I met over a mix-up at a laundromat close to my apartment. I mistook her dryer for mine and mine for hers. We laughed and traded items as we talked and folded. We ran into each other almost weekly doing laundry."

"Not a bad beginning." Carla finished her water. She put her glass in the sink and put two bowls on the table. "Sort berries while we talk?"

Kirk got up, pulled the wastebasket to the table, and pulled a basket of berries to him. "A good start to a friendship. We had lunch, dinner and a few movies from time to time. When the consortium I worked for closed, several businesses started laying people off. Diana and I pooled our resources and moved in together as friends. Her family took it we were engaged and announced it as such. Fast forward some. Diana's grandfather shows up at our door with a matchmaker, state justice of the peace and a partially filled-out marriage license."

"The proverbial manure hit the fan?" Daniel asked, setting a plate of cheese and crackers on the table.

Kirk laughed. "Our families didn't want to hear anything different. Six months into an eighteen-month lease, we jumped the broom, declared our interests, and filed the state paperwork. Ten months later, we found out the state had nullified the paperwork. The matchmaker wasn't licensed to perform unions in Tennessee."

"Shit ton of fertilizer hitting brick wall." Carla got up hugged Kirk and refilled everyone's water glass.

"Surplus for sure." Kirk tossed the empty berry basket in the trash, popped a cracker and cheese in his mouth and chewed. He swallowed, drank some water and tapped on the table. "The kicker to all this was Diana's divorce from her first spouse never finalized. She was in process of getting back together with her when all this manure went down. The marriage was a farce from the get-go."

"Damn Kirk. I knew the Diana thing was nasty. Not that nasty. I'm sorry, bro." Daniel washed the berries, added sugar to the bowls and stirred. "Berry shortcake for dessert tonight. Grilled steaks and baked potatoes for dinner. Lunch is Hodge Podge Soup."

"*Not Hodge Podge Soup*," Kirk groaned. "Every supernatural family has that recipe in their family cookbook. Pull it out of the freezer, fridge, and cupboard. Thaw it, open it, and chop it up. 'Cuz in the pot it's going."

Carla stood, walked to the cabinet she'd gotten the mugs out of earlier, opened it and pulled out four cans. "Hodge Podge Gourmet Soup coming up."

"Fancifying the name ain't gonna change the mix." Kirk examined the four cans. "What else you putting in the pot?"

"You got French cut green beans, peas, carrots and we can spare a couple of potatoes that are sprouting eyes. Daniel what meat you got in the freezer besides steaks?" Carla started opening cans.

"Fancy-cut vegetables don't make the soup gourmet." Kirk followed Daniel to the freezer.

"No it doesn't. I got some wine that needs using. Too bitter to drink but great in a pot of stew or soup. Might be some stew beef or lamb chunks. How about both?" Daniel held up two small packages of meat.

"Drunk soup, decent meat, and vegetables. . ." Kirk cocked his head left and right. "Berry shortcake later on. Daniel order up a couple gallons of the best ice cream the grocery has and a couple bottles of chocolate sauce. I'll split the bill with you later."

"I keep forgetting your stomach is a bottomless pit at times." Daniel hastily scribbled items on the pad on the side of the fridge.

"One of you strong men can carry these into the laundry room." Carla stacked the laundry baskets, one on top of the other." I'll get the wash started while you decide what else you're ordering from the grocery."

Kirk hefted the baskets, making motions like they were filled with rocks. "Who thought all these clothes we wear could weigh so much."

Daniel plopped the pad on the table and dropped into the chair closest to him. "Wonder if the hardware store is open. Could use a shovel and several buckets to clean out the fertilizer piles."

"Duly noted," Kirk called out, entering the laundry room. "You might need a few dozen mops to clean up too."

Carla dumped the open cans in the large pot Daniel had set on the counter as they rummaged in the cabinet for possible soup ingredients. She tossed the empty cans in the trash as she walked by Daniel. "Daniel, thaw the meat, please, while I help Kirk with the laundry."

Kirk sat the baskets on the floor. He turned as Carla entered the laundry room. "Kiss for a hard-working man?"

Carla shook her finger at him. "Not until your work's done. Show me where the detergent and softener are."

Kirk started opening the cabinets close to him. "How am I supposed to know? Ask Daniel. It's his place."

Carla elbowed him as she opened the cabinet over the washer. "Kirk, if we're family, isn't each of our places everybody's?"

"Yeah, I guess." Kirk set a bottle of laundry detergent on the washer. "Isn't that one of those future questions?"

"Could be. Each of us brings part of who we are to this mix." Carla measured detergent and softener into the washer, added the first load, and pushed the start button.

"Territorial is porous?" Kirk set the second basket on the dryer and faced Carla.

"More like we mix at certain points and others we're are own person." Carla laid her hand on his arm. "We've got things to work out. This isn't a one-and-done."

Kirk leaned closer to Carla. "Are you saying you're willing to give us a try?"

Carla shrugged. "I'm saying we've got boundaries. Experiences and need to knows."

"More talk?" Kirk kissed Carla's cheek and stepped past her.

"Communicate, communicate, and more." Carla nodded. "We can play catch up or build a foundation."

Kirk sighed and exited the laundry room. Had they started on the foundation?

Daniel looked up as Kirk entered the kitchen. "What flavor ice cream you want?"

Kirk opened the freezer, shut it and plopped in a chair. "Neapolitan and whatever you and Carla want. This isn't just about me."

Carla checked the soup, added the meat, and stirred. She turned the burner to simmer. "Wash started. I'm good with peach or mixed berries. Can put some of the berry mix over it."

Daniel pushed the list to the center of the table. "I'll call the order in after lunch. I'm good with telling my catch-up part."

"Sure, go ahead." Carla refilled her water and sat next to Kirk.

"Listening." Kirk popped a cracker and cheese into his mouth and chewed.

Daniel flipped the pad over, tore off a blank sheet of paper and laid it middle of the table. He drew a triangle, a circle around the triangle and then a square around the circle and triangle. "You know my family's triangular view about protecting male witches and the circle of protective relatives I got to associate with. Square was the boundary my family tried to impose. Part of the reason I fled to Europe was to break free."

"Our families fenced themselves in." Carla picked up a cracker and cheese. "Isolation. Purity of species. What the hell were they trying to prove?"

"My theory is they were scared. Too scared to admit being fearful." Daniel pulled the grocery pad to him. "Last part of my catch-up is I fell in lust quick, thought Rachel was the one and proposed. Thirty-eight days into the marriage, Rachel disappeared. I got a letter with annulment papers from a top divorce attorney. Second time I thought I found the one, I walked away before the vows exchange. Lisa's family kept voicing why she and I shouldn't get married."

"Guess that leaves me." Carla walked to the stove, stirred the soup, and walked back to the table.

CHAPTER FOURTEEN

"My parents' purist attitudes caught me by surprise. Picked me up from school and kept driving until we reached Witchery. A tiny, tiny blip on the Nevada map. Town's ruling enclave and school board insisted on genome testing for me and my siblings. Genetic markings placed you in what school and classes you went to. Labeled slow and NMW left me isolated and on my own. I made a few friends who taught me sleight-of-hand tricks magicians use." Carla leaned back in her chair.

"NMW?" Daniel stopped writing and looked up. "Slow? How so?"

"You tutored us. Tutored me in algebra, chemistry and financial literacy. You got me interested in accounting and business." Kirk stared at her. His mouth open.

"NMW is not a magical witch. My recessive genes are witch ones. My more dominant genes are mortal." Carla leaned forward, resting her elbows on the table. "My parents insisted on testing me five more times. The geneticist told them after the fifth time. They needed testing to see which one of them had mortal genes."

"Oh holy crap twice over. Bet that set off aura fireworks and not in a good way." Kirk stood and stretched. "I'm glad you escaped. Ran away or whatever it took to get you away from there."

"I'm sorry you went through that." Daniel leaned over and hugged her tightly.

"After while, I didn't mind. I got into advanced basic magician classes and other practical learning. A friend, her boyfriend and I left town on pretext of running errands next town over two hours away. We kept going and never looked back. Rafe and Anita dropped me at Aunt Moriah's and continued their elopement. Often wonder if they ever made it to their final destination. They never said what it was." Carla returned Daniel's hug. "Ready to call the order in?"

"Soup first. Order second. I heard the washer chime. Load is done." Daniel set bowls and spoons on the counter. Next to them the soup ladle.

"I think we've laid four foundation cornerstones." Kirk placed the soup pot on the counter. "First cornerstone, we're together again. Filling in missing pieces and strengthening our connections."

Daniel handed a bowl of soup and a spoon to Carla. "Second, third and fourth cornerstones are each of us. Sharing ourselves, being ourselves and interconnecting who we are with each other."

Carla sat next to Kirk. "The cement or glue is our friendship and connection. I think we're ready to move to the next communication level. Dating? Intimacy? What's next?"

Kirk added crackers and cheese to his soup and mixed it. Some of the things they'd discussed were known bits and pieces. Things friends and acquaintances knew or told them. Shower play was flirting. Naked flirting. A nice distraction. Occupied his psyche rather well. His ankle twinged off and on during the night. He hadn't favored it stepping in and out of the shower. Asking Daniel what painkillers he had in stock would let that secret out. Bad shoulder. Bad ankle. Shifted at will. Sometimes without notice if pain got high enough. Then there was howling. Not loud. Just enough to notify pain was pinging and hammering through him. Kirk looked up. Daniel and Carla's gaze met his. "Sorry thought rambling."

"No problem." Daniel held up his glass. "Here's to us. Communication happening. Building on our strong four cornerstone foundation."

Kirk touched his glass to Daniel's and Carla's. Would the foundation withstand more revealed secrets?

Kirk finished his second bowl of soup. He pushed back from the table, gripping the table's edge, and tried to stand. Pain lanced through him upwards in sharp spurts, grappling its climb with deeper lashes the longer he stood. He dropped back in the chair. He let go a deep sigh. He slumped back in the chair as he spoke. "Daniel, what painkillers you got?"

Daniel put his dishes down on the table. "How bad is it?"

"Not howl worthy yet. Hadn't picked up my prescription refill. I guess I overdid it." Kirk glanced at Carla. "Guess I'll reveal the next level of secrets. Don't blame you if this turns you off."

"Your secret can wait. You need help." Carla refilled his water glass. "What do you need?"

"Ice pack. My cane out of my truck. And a pain-killing pill or two." Kirk grimaced, trying to pull another chair to him and lift his ankle.

"Hang tight, buddy. I've got arthritis strength or migraine strength OTCs. Which you want?" Daniel opened the cabinet next to the sink and pulled out two bottles.

"Two arthritis strength and help with getting my ankle propped up." Kirk leaned on the table, panting. Pain level was an eight out of eleven. He wasn't going to hit howling eleven if he could help it.

Carla pushed a chair tight to his. "Need help lifting your ankle?"

"Please." Kirk leaned back, fisted the leg of his jeans in his hand, and tugged upward.

Carla positioned the chair, slipped a hand under his calf and held his leg steady.

"Thanks. A bit to the right." Kirk captured his top lip between his teeth and worked them back and forth, trying to distract his subconscious focus. "Daniel, push the chair cattycornered to me. Carla, slowly slide your hands up to my knee."

Kirk let go of his jeans, pressed his teeth tight to his lip and groaned. He slowly exhaled, blinked and gave Daniel and Carla two thumbs up. "Sorry."

Carla started stuffing ice in the plastic bag Daniel had put on the counter. "Sorry for what? Needing help? Asking for it?"

Kirk held out his hand, palm up. Daniel shook two pills out and set the bottle and cap on the table next to the water glass. "Why didn't you say something sooner? I'd gotten your cane for you."

Kirk downed the two pills, emptied the water glass, and set it on the table. "Emotional haze. Feeling good. Ankle hadn't bothered me most of the week. Mind on other things."

"Daniel, he needs a towel wrapped around this." Carla laid the plastic bag full of ice on the table. "Do you need a pillow or anything else under your ankle?"

"Maybe a second towel. And more water." Kirk held up his glass. "Ten minutes of ice and the pills will corral the pain gremlins. I'll need to walk around some once that happens. Blood flow thing."

"I'll get your cane in a moment." Daniel sat across from him. "I think you need to tell Carla about this."

Carla sat next to him holding his hand. "Please. I need to understand. I want to know."

"Daniel's right, Carla. You should know about this." Kirk drank a third of his water. "You know my dad was in the Air Force. I signed up for ROTC to help finish paying for college. One weekend a month, I went for training. Dad talked about paratroopers' school. He brought home the enrollment forms signed by him and his commander." Kirk winced and gulped more of his water.

"Painful memory?' Carla let go of his hand and got him more water. "You can tell me about it at another time."

"Ankle pinged. Lingering pain killer tablet taste in my mouth." Kirk let out a burp. "Not much more to tell. I fell off the training platform landing on my ankle with my arms wrapped around the platform support pole. Wracked my shoulder up again. Shoulder brace eight months. Ankle sprained and torn Achilles tendon. Surgery to correct both. Earned myself family nickname Klutz."

Daniel set a bowl of berries in front of him. Kirk looked up. "Why?"

"You survived. You told the tale. None of us is running out the door." Daniel laid a spoon and napkin next to the bowl. "First attempts in learning never guarantee success. You went on to graduate with honors. Opened a successful business. Are you happy?"

"Depends on happy definition." Kirk ate two spoonfuls of berries. He swallowed and continued his train of thought. "Lately I've been thinking about whose definition I'm measuring things by. The one Klutz had shoved down his throat. Was taunted by and ridiculed relentlessly by bullies and so-called family members."

Carla plucked a berry out of his bowl, popped it in her mouth, and kissed his cheek. She perched on his lap, looping her arms around his shoulders and neck, steadying herself. "Here's the secret you think you had to keep. You fouled up. Messed up. Fucked up someone else's standards and plans for you. Not your plans. You turned the incident into a win. You told me in a letter you found time to think about what you wanted to do. You found what got you juicy mentally. That's a huge win. Like Daniel said, you found you."

Kirk slipped his arm around Carla's waist, hugged her and let go. "Need both hands for berry eating and steadying. Don't need to fall off the chair."

Carla carefully stood and stepped away from Kirk. "Sorry, I didn't keep track of time. Iced your ankle for fifteen minutes instead of ten."

Daniel plucked the bag and towel off as he passed the chair propping up Kirk's ankle. "I'm going to get your cane. Then run to the store to pick up what we need. Is easier and quicker than calling an order in. Carla, I think you can kiss and make better anywhere Kirk needs it."

Carla opened her mouth to retort. She caught Daniel's wink as he opened the back door. "I sure can. Kirk and I can make a list of what needs kissing and massaging. Take your time at the grocery. We'll be just fine. Right, Kirk?"

Kirk shot her a puzzled look. "Kiss? Make better? Massaging?"

"I'll explain in a few. Maybe show you too. Is there anything else we need Daniel to add to the list?" Carla nibbled Kirk's neck. She pulled back. Was Kirk flushing?

Daniel closed the door, whistling as he did.

Kirk turned toward Carla as best he could. "Did Daniel just toss me at you? Tell you to have your way with me?"

"Oh, could be." Carla trailed her fingers down Kirk's chest, past the waist of his shorts, stopping as she reached the bottom of his zipper, close to his cock and balls.

"Ah, you're not going to tie me up and have your way with me, are you?" Kirk gulped the last of his water.

"Just because I practiced my magic knot trick on you and it backfired doesn't mean I haven't practiced." Carla picked up his glass. "You look a mite parched. More water?"

"At this rate, I'm gonna need a shower, all the ice in the freezer and a dozen condoms." Kirk clasped the glass. His hand and fingers close to Carla's. The glass showed evidence of steam marks already happening.

Daniel rapped on the backdoor twice with Kirk's cane. From his quick peek through the door window, a planning conversation appeared to be happening. He opened the door, calling out as he did. "No TMI needed. No permission needed. Clean up your mess afterward. Clean sheets are in the hall closet. I'm off to the grocery."

"Aren't you glad you got a one-story house?" Kirk replied.

Daniel laid Kirk's cane on the table, thoroughly kissed Carla goodbye and grabbed his keys off the key rack next to the door. "Makes chasing each other easier, I guess. And by the way, there's no rope anywhere in the house. Traditional old-fashioned fun is probably your best options."

Carla dropped into the chair across from Kirk, laughing and wiping tears at the same time.

CHAPTER FIFTEEN

"I'm glad there's *no* rope in the house," Kirk muttered, wrapping his hands around his calf. He carefully swung his leg off the chair and lowered it. Carla kept watching him. She wasn't going to pounce unexpectedly. Kirk tipped back his head, opened his mouth and let out a mournful howl.

"Deities on high, Kirk!" Carla jumped and trotted toward him. "Are you in pain?"

"Take it easy, Carla. I'm fine." Kirk rubbed his hands together gleefully. "Got ya!"

"Kirk Addison, that wasn't nice." Carla pinched his ass cheeks twice.

"Ouch! *That* wasn't nice." Kirk rubbed his ass cheeks with both hands. "Was making sure my howler was in working order."

"Howler?" Carla moved his cane closer to him.

"Letting off some steam. Pain isn't close to pleasure for me." Kirk leaned on the table, stood, hopping on his good foot, and reached for his cane. "We pranked each other good, sweetie. How about some kisses and make-up cuddles?"

Carla glowered at him, her hands on her hips. "I'm deciding who kisses what to make better and who's first."

Kirk captured his retort before he blurted it out. Joint kisses and making better cuddles didn't include who went first or second or even where it all began. Puppy pile of arms, hands, lips and other parts close and pressed against each other was an apt description.

"How about we call it a draw?" Kirk clasped his cane and straightened. "We each get to decide where the other gets to kiss and make better first?"

Carla lowered her hands, sighed and moved the chairs out of their way. "Make-out cuddles are awesome. Do we get naked first or play kiss and make better strip?"

"First person on the bed decides." Kirk hobbled toward the living room. He made his way around the couch and coffee table, glancing over his shoulder. Carla was right behind him. He entered the hallway leading to the bedroom, "Ready—set—go!"

"Kirk, you think a headstart is going to help you?" Carla caught up with him and pinched his ass again.

"Stop that." Kirk paused at the bedroom door. "Who's not playing fair now?"

Carla stood toe to toe with him. She leaned close and whispered, "*Neither of us.*"

Kirk snickered, turned and hobbled into the bedroom, tossed his cane into the wingback chair and dropped on the bed tittering. "Double score on that one. One for you. One for me. Our misbehaving score is tied."

Carla shucked her top and tossed it toward the chair. It landed on top of his cane. She undid the front clasp of her bra. "I'm going to win the stripping contest. You haven't even started yet."

"Oh, I've started. I started enjoying the show mere moments ago." Kirk pulled his shirt over his head, tossed it at Carla and lay back on the bed.

Carla caught Kirk's shirt, tossing it over her shoulder, barely noting where it landed. She pushed her bra straps off her shoulders, down her arms and dropped it where she stood. Kirk leaned back on the bed on his elbows watching her. He fisted part of the blanket in each hand. Her gaze roved lower. Down to where Kirk's groin and crotch met. There was no mistaking the bulge that pushed the shorts fly up. She was getting to him.

She tugged one side of her jeans lower. Then, the other side. Each crept back up as she tugged them up and down. Carla undid her belt. She advanced a couple of steps. "Should I stop? Or help you strip?"

Kirk reached down, pulling his shorts away from his crotch. Oh, she was getting to him good. She remembered what Daniel and Kirk had told her about guys signaling they were interested and turned on. Pulling their pants away from their groin and crotch area signaled one thing. Their cock and balls were very interested in what was happening.

Kirk sat up. "I suppose we could even things up. Your shirt is off. Mine is off. What's next?"

Carla undid her jeans, unzipped the zipper halfway, and held out her hand. Kirk grasped her hand and tugged her to him. Carla stumbled forward, putting her other hand out, hoping to halt her fall.

Their combined momentum bounced them as they tumbled onto the bed. Kirk on his back. Her between his legs. Their bare upper torsos plastered against each other. Not even a hair's width between them. Their chests practically rose and fell in unison. Carla held her breath. Kirk's chest rose and fell as he inhaled and exhaled. She exhaled slowly. Whoever said bare flesh on bare flesh wasn't sexy and didn't ignite chemistry didn't know what the hell they were talking about. This beat out all their earlier shower play. Topped it. Pushed it over the top.

"I love being like this," Kirk whispered in her ear. "*But* if you move too quickly, I'm out of commission."

"Huh?" Carla tried to push herself up.

"Stay still." Kirk let go of her arm. "I'll help you stand up. Prefer your knee and my balls don't meet up."

Carla nodded. "Palm to palm. My palm on yours, and you help push me up? I step back once I'm upright?"

"Yes!" Kirk held out his hands, palms up toward her. "Not too quick. Ready?"

Carla laid her palms on Kirk's. "Ready."

Kirk pushed up, pushing Carla up and off him. Trickles of cool air fluttered over his chest. Carla shifted slightly. Her outer thigh brushed his thigh. He glanced between them. There was space growing bit by bit. "Just a bit more."

Carla nodded. "I'm going to step back with my leg closest to your balls."

Kirk pressed his lips together. The next steps would be the most delicate ones. It was going to take careful teamwork. "Easy does it. One step then another."

Carla let go of his hands. Kirk lowered his arms and slid his hands down as far as he could, hoping he covered his balls and cock. Carla moved one leg back, then her other until cool air rushed up over his hands. Kirk swallowed, looked down and exhaled. They'd done it. Saved his cock and balls. Carla deserved one heck of a thank-you orgasm.

"It's time for shared clothes shucking. You help me and I help you." Kirk sat up, reaching for the waistband of Carla's jeans.

Carla laid her hands on Kirk's. "Together is easier."

Down over her hips, her panties and jeans went. Past her knees and onto the floor, pooling around her feet. She stood nude before Kirk again. This time, there was no hesitancy. No fear of being caught. No time was of the essence.

They were here now because they wanted to be. Shivers rushed over her as Kirk gave her a hot up-and-down checkout.

"Definitely like what I unwrapped and see," Kirk growled low in his throat.

Previously, Kirk's growl scared her. Not now. She knew without words what he told her. Accepted her, wanted her and enjoyed the view she presented him. Deeper into her inner core, his next low growl flooded. Her wolfish Kirk was letting his mate know he claimed her and their mating dance was starting.

Carla kicked her jeans away. She moved to Kirk's right, kneeling beside him. She worked her hand past the waistband of his shorts until the waistband prevented her sliding her hand down farther past his navel. She leaned down, pressed her lips against Kirk's stomach and licked. Saltiness rushed over her taste buds and rapidly disappeared. Would his semen taste the same or better? She raised her head. Kirk's gaze met hers. He nodded, reaching for the shorts fly button and zipper. Her hand covered Kirk's. Together, they worked the zipper open. Kirk unbuttoned his shorts with his other hand.

Carla wrapped her arm around Kirk's waist as he leaned on his cane. "You work the other side down once I've got this side down."

"Thanks. I really appreciate your help." Kirk moved his cane to his other hand. "Not many women would get this far with me."

"Why?" Carla asked, working the waist of Kirk's shorts and briefs past his hip on her side. "You need help. We all do at some point. Not like it makes you any less desirable."

"That's the problem." Kirk shifted his cane back to his other hand. "Survival of the fittest. Women see the cane and think damaged goods. They only see the outside. Never get to know me in here." Kirk touched his chest close to his heart.

Carla rose up on her tiptoes and kissed Kirk's cheek. " I so get what you're talking about. People , even our own families, not seeing us. Not valuing us. It hurts. Hurts real damn bad."

"You sure you want to continue?" Kirk gripped his shorts and briefs waistbands.

Carla cupped Kirk's cheek, nodding as she placed her hand on his and spoke. "*Oh yeah.* I know and see all of you. Shapeshifter, wolf and human. I know the heart and mind pretty good of the man I'm going to be intimate with."

Kirk pushed his shorts and briefs off his hip. The side next to Carla followed. He looked down. There was no mistaking his arousal. His cock stuck out wanting to see more. Know more. Feel Carla's touch and caress again.

"Let's get you completely out of these." Carla knelt beside him, lifted one foot, then his other. She tossed his shorts and briefs over her shoulder at the wingback chair. Kirk smiled, seeing where they landed on top of their other cast-aside clothing.

Kirk pointed at himself. "Chemistry ignited."

"I want to taste you." Carla softly lifted his balls with one hand. Encircled his cock with her other and leaned forward, her lips open ready for her taste.

Warm wetness slid across his glans. Flicking licks. Slow laving suckles as Carla took more of him into her mouth. She swallowed him partway down to where her hand held him. Her fingers found the spot at the base of his balls, close to his scrotum. The magical male spot almost equal to her clitoris. He jerked as Carla sucked him more. Oral sex was a goodness. It wasn't the way he wanted their first loving orgasm to happen. Carla's pleasure mattered.

"Sweetie," Kirk managed to say, in between delicious jolts of pleasure inching their way up and down his cock, settling in his balls, and overflowing to his male external g spot. "Don't know if I can manage twice. Too turned on. Want inside you. Pleasure you."

Carla slid Kirk out of her mouth, lowered her hand, and rose. "You taste awesome. Thank you for being a giving lover. What position works for you?"

Kirk backed up against the bed and dropped on it. His cane clattered on the floor. "Sorry. Distracted and needing to think at same time, not quite happening."

Carla laid the cane on the bed. Her hand slid up Kirk's thigh stopping close to his hard-on. "Glad I could distract you that good. Need question reminder?"

"Need your answer." Kirk laced his fingers in her hair and pulled her to him.

His lips met hers, parted, and his tongue gave chase, seeking to taste her. Sip from her as he tossed more embers on her intense smoldering flames. Kirk cupped her breast, tracing her areola and nipple with his thumb. Over, around and back in short flicks and longer strokes mimicking what she'd done to him. Every pulse rushed down into her, deeper until her clit countered the rhythm her nipples throbbed with.

Carla pulled back, breaking off the kiss. She walked over to the nightstand, opened the condom box and took a condom packet out. She held it up as she made her way back to Kirk. "I get STD tested every three months. Food Council requirement. No STDs, no illness in the last year, and I'm on the pill. Using condoms is a great way to protect both of us. You?"

"No illness. Last STD test six months ago. General check-up. Glad you protect yourself. Condoms are necessary protection. Nothing is a hundred percent." Kirk scooted back on the bed. "Sides or on top?"

"On top." Carla tore open the condom packet. "Easier to get this on and our pleasure started."

Kirk lay on his back, stroking his cock. "Great position for double orgasms for you. So enjoyed stroking your clit earlier."

Carla leaned down, flicked her tongue across Kirk's glans and suckled him in her mouth, wetting a third of him. She worked the condom down and over him until her fingers met his, where he held his cock close to his balls. She stepped back, admired her handiwork and knelt on the bed. "It's time. Time for pleasure."

She straddled Kirk's waist. He reached between them, rubbing his hand down her stomach until he reached her mons. He blew her a kiss and nodded. "I'm ready. Ready and very able to pleasure both of us."

Carla moved back, halting when she felt Kirk rub against her. His cock close to her clitoris. Back and forth, she gently rocked, positioning herself. She clasped Kirk, holding him steady as she inserted him.

"Ahh" Kirk moaned. "Much better than any dream."

Carla closed her eyes and rocked forward. Kirk was in her. Balls deep as she heard one of her cousins describe how he loved to do it. She rocked back, setting a steady slow rhythm. There was no hurry. No rush.

Kirk slicked his fingers with Carla's wetness. Positioned them so each rock forward or backward, he stroked her clitoris. Deep within her inner heat, he basked. Deep where he'd imagined being and dreamt about. Now their mutual pleasure was close to exploding.

Carla picked up the pace of her rocking. His balls tightened to him. Her clitoris swelled. He licked the fingers of his other hand and captured her nipple. Tugging it in counter thrust to her rocking. Could he withstand much more?

"*Oh, Kirk,*" Carla cried out. "*I'm there. I'm there.*"

Wetness flowed onto his hand as he continued stroking Carla's clitoris. She tightened around him, squeezing him every time her clitoris pulsed. Kirk thrust up, stiffened and let out a low growling howl. "I'm there now."

Carla helped him pull out, keeping the condom on. She collapsed beside him. Her hand lay close to his. Neither of them spoke for several minutes.

"Wow," Carla said, rolling on her side toward him.

"Double wow," Kirk managed to get out in between breaths. "Give me a few moments. I'll be okay."

"I don't think either of us is moving for a bit." Carla eased onto her back.

Kirk laid his hand on her stomach. "Many more sparks and we'd set off the smoke detector."

Carla glanced at Kirk who stuck his tongue out of his mouth sideways and rolled his eyes back and forth. She pressed her lips together. Her smile refused being suppressed.

Kirk chortled and sat up. "Change sheets or clean up first?"

"Clean up, dress and then sheets. Daniel can help if he gets back in time." Carla sauntered toward the bathroom. Kirk right behind her.

Kirk slipped the condom off, keeping hold of the semen-filled tip. He held the condom up. "No tears. No apparent leaks."

Carla turned the faucet on. "Run water in it. Best way to test for possible tears or leaks."

Kirk filled the condom twice and emptied it. "No tears or leaks, I can see."

"Same here." Carla tossed the condom in the toilet and flushed. "Clean up time."

"We messed up the sheets. Not Daniel." Kirk stepped into the shower, turned it on and ducked under the spray.

Carla handed Kirk the soap and moved past him to wet down. "True. But he gave us the idea. Planted the seed."

Kirk handed her the soap as he moved past her to rinse off. "Maybe we change only the ones we messed up. Like the top sheet?"

Carla soaped, put the soap in the shower soap dish and rinsed as Kirk exited the shower. "Daniel didn't say which sheets to put on. We could use whatever we find."

Kirk chortled louder. "Mix and match. Can't say we didn't follow through."

"Exactly." Carla hung her towel next to Kirk's and followed him out of the bathroom.

CHAPTER SIXTEEN

Daniel set the grocery bags on the counter. No sign of Carla or Kirk. Probably snoozing. Post-orgasmic bliss kicked in. He'd deliberately taken the long way back. Kirk and Carla deserved time. Time to do whatever they did. Daniel hoped it was intimate and good for both of them.

Compersion wasn't always easy. Having joy because your loved ones were experiencing joy sometimes required focused effort. He wasn't jealous. Envious sorta described what he felt as he pulled out of the drive. Truth knocked him upside the head as he pulled into the shopping plaza parking lot. He wanted things to work out. Wanted so bad he could taste it. Taste the bittersweet doubt that his past failed relationships ignited when he considered trying again. Enough doubt, memory lane chases and flashbacks. There were more items in the trunk of the car he needed help bringing in.

Daniel put the last of the perishables in the fridge and glanced at the clock. Six-fifteen P.M. Steaks needed a half hour to marinate. Grill took thirty minutes to heat up. Baked potatoes ala microwave fifteen minutes for three. Seven-thirty dinner time might work. The only way he was going to know if Carla and Kirk were sleeping or awake was to check. Daniel shook out his hands. Pushed the picture his second sight kept flashing at him away and made his way to the bedroom. Did he call out or knock or both before opening the door?

He stopped as he reached the bedroom door. It was ajar. Moans and groans creeped around the door and out into the hall. Shit, what had he almost walked in on? Voyeurism wasn't his thing. Threesomes might turn some people on. Not him. Their group shower play and threesome makeout were different than trying to coordinate tab A into slot B and make sure everybody fitted together or got their pleasure meter punched. Daniel swallowed hard, turned ready to retreat to the kitchen and rethink dinner plans.

"Ahh. More. Harder," Kirk's voice called. "Carla, where did you learn that?"

Carla's laughter followed. "Look it up on the internet. Search engine."

Kirk's deep groan sounded, followed by joint laughter.

Daniel turned back, ready to push the door open and call Kirk and Carla out for spoofing him.

"My friend Alethea is a massage therapist specializing in acupuncture and acupressure massage. She taught me the points that help with releasing tight muscles and the amount of pressure needed." Carla opened the bedroom door. "Hey Daniel!"

Daniel opened his mouth and closed it. Carla and Kirk were dressed. The bed...the sheets didn't match. His to-do list shrunk.

Kirk stretched, worked his arms up and down, picked up his cane and stood. "Carla gives one hell of a good shoulder massage. Found the trigger points and got them to release."

Carla tugged on Daniel's arm. She tipped her head back. Lips puckered. Daniel glanced from Kirk to Carla. Shook his head and kissed Carla. Skepticism-one. Vivid imagination-a thousand plus. Compersion-a drip in the bucket filling with more drips fast.

Carla looped her arms around Daniel's waist and hugged him. "Kirk and I were haved. You did tell us to behave."

Daniel pressed his lips together. More than once his sisters had shinnied up into Carla's cousins' treehouse telling Kirk, Carla and him to behave. The joke was on all of them since the ladder for the treehouse was up inside it thanks to him and Kirk pulling it up behind them. No wonder he enjoyed misbehaving more. Daniel snickered watching Carla saunter away from him. Kirk patted him on the shoulder and followed Carla out of the room.

Carla leaned against the kitchen counter. Neither she nor Kirk had planned to pull a joke on Daniel. Kirk's shoulder caught twice as they made love. Carla gripped the counter. She used the L word. The L-O-V-E word. She pressed her palms tighter on the counter. Kirk had told her twice he loved her massage. Why did the word make her twinge? Or did it?

Daniel entered the kitchen. "You two got me good."

Kirk grinned. "Wasn't planned."

Carla let go of the counter and turned. "Didn't know you were back."

Daniel pointed at her and Kirk. "No you didn't. Didn't want to interrupt bellowing I'm home."

Snickers and smirks followed by more laughter erupted. Kirk pulled out a chair, laid his cane on the table and dropped into the chair. "Blasted shoulder decided to make its presence felt during our lovefest."

"Least I could do was return the favor giving it pleasure. A few oohs and aahs of its own you know." Carla gave Kirk a quick hug and walked over to Daniel. "I can ink you in for tonight."

Kirk cleared his throat. "Only if we get the guest room inhabitable. Bed made and bathroom necessities stocked."

"Let me check my calendar." Daniel pulled his cell phone out. Acted like he was scrolling through his calendar. He looked up, catching Kirk's gaze. Kirk nodded and gave him a thumbs up. "Okay, got room. You're invitation accepted. You're inked in."

Carla rubbed her hands together. "Excellent. What's for dinner?"

"Earlier menu as decided. Steaks grilled, baked potatoes ala microwave and berry shortcake with ice cream from Galperson's." Daniel snugged Carla to him and let go.

Kirk pushed back from the table. "You did get the *good stuff*."

"Mrs. Galperson said you owed her grandson Nicholas something. I said I'd deliver the message." Daniel set a bowl on the counter and began mixing the marinade. "Anything I can help with?"

"Nicholas is interested in accounting and is up for Shifter Leader Scout award. Told him I would see about an internship for him." Kirk got the steaks out of the fridge. He laid them on the counter next to the marinade bowl. "Daniel, you or I starting the grill?"

"I see why Uncle Zac appointed you two co-alphas." Carla poured the shortcake batter into a baking pan and put it in the oven. "Community connections, respected, and great reputations."

"I hope we can do as good a job." Daniel unwrapped the steaks. He layered them in the marinade and put the bowl back in the fridge. "I'm starting the grill. Don't need a blast furnace cooking the steaks."

"Okay, I fucked up with pouring lighter fluid on the charcoal grill at our senior cookout. That was ten years ago." Kirk folded his arms across his chest and stared squinty-eyed at Daniel.

"True. My grill is gas. No lighter fluid or charcoal needed. I know the grill's idiocracies." Daniel rinsed his hands and opened the back door. "You and Carla can get the rest of the stuff out of my trunk. Paint supplies."

Kirk groaned. "Not the neon pink you threatened."

Daniel laughed. "You'll have to wait and see."

Kirk grabbed his cane off the table and Daniel's car keys off the pegboard by the door. "Come on Carla. Let's see what we're up against."

Carla glanced at Daniel, drew three lines in the air, and followed Kirk out the garage door. Daniel started whistling and went out the back door.

Kirk opened Daniel's car trunk. Four boxes from the local hardware store filled one-half of the trunk. The other half held seven paint cans. Kirk grabbed a handle, held the can up, and read the label aloud. "Aqua for hall bath."

"Not neon pink." Carla picked up a can and read the label out loud. "Periwinkle for C's room."

"Oh, Lupa, he did it." Kirk set the can he held on the garage floor. He checked the labels on the remaining cans. "Primer and beige. We're safe."

"The beige says for K's room." Carla set the can she held next to the one Kirk put on the floor. "What did Daniel do?"

"There's four bedrooms including the master. Daniel declared it his room. He's giving you and me are own rooms." Kirk picked up two of the paint cans out of the trunk. "We've got a second home."

"A what?" Carla gawked quizzically at Kirk.

"An additional safe place. Another place called home. Our own space within." Kirk chortled gleefully. "Daniel and I agreed we wanted and needed a place where the three of us could come together and feel that same way. Know we were wanted, could be ourselves and hole up as needed."

"How could you know I'd agree to come here? Be intimate with you and agree to be intimate with Daniel?" Carla picked up two of the paint cans off the garage floor and followed Kirk into the house.

"We didn't. We took a chance that what we had was still strong and that our friendship was still alive." Kirk stopped where the hall split toward the opposite back side of the house. "Set the cans and boxes along the wall. We get to decide which room we want."

Carla peered down the hall. At the end of the hall, she could make out the porcelain tub and sliding shower doors. The hall bath. On one side, there were two open doors and a third on the opposite side. "Are the rooms all the same size?"

Kirk pointed at the two open doors on the same side. "Those two are. Daniel thought about making one of those the guest room."

"And the other?" Carla started down the hall.

"Not quite as large as the master suite. There's potential for enlarging the room. Maybe making another master suite. Depends on what we want to do with the place." Kirk pushed open the door to the room.

Carla entered. Sunlight poured in through the two windows on the front side of the house. She turned taking in the room's positioning. Not as square as Daniel's room. More like an odd-shaped rectangle. Along the back wall, doors to the walk-in closet were open. She turned toward the door and Kirk. "This room has definite potential. Almost could put a den and bedroom in here."

"It does," Daniel said, walking into the room. "Thought about making it into the guest room and home office. If it's our home, we get to decide what goes in here."

Carla entwined her hand with Daniel's. She held her other out to Kirk. Kirk clasped her hand. Carla raised their joined hands. "I declare this house our refuge. Our dwelling. Here is where we are family reunited."

Daniel moved and turned closer to Kirk. He held out his hand to Kirk.

Kirk leaned his cane against his leg, took hold of Daniel's hand, raised their joined hands and spoke, "I am reunited with my family here. Here is safe space for us to gather and be ourselves. This house is our safe haven."

Keeping their hands raised, Daniel stepped into the circle closer to Carla and Kirk. "We are a family of three. Our asylum is here. Our reunion always begins here."

Carla and Kirk stepped into the circle. They let go of their hands, put their arms around each other's waist, and moved into a group hug.

"Yellows and reds around us flash," Daniel whispered.

Kirk murmured the next line. "Colors of passion mauve and lavender unite."

"Show us our family aura as we unite." Carla closed her eyes, hoping her latent magic would ignite the catalyst needed to display their union aura.

A buzzing sound echoed in the hall. Carla sniffed. "Oh, crap, the shortcake."

Carla bolted out of the room. Daniel and Kirk following her.

Carla shut off the timer, grabbed a potholder and opened the oven. Delightful aromas wafted out of the oven. Carla set the done to a golden brown shortcake on the stove. She turned the oven off as another timer started buzzing. "I swear I didn't set the smoke detector off."

"Grill timer." Daniel picked up the timer setting on the counter. He got the marinade bowl out of the fridge. "Time to start the steaks. Kirk, will you get the potatoes ready?"

"Sure will." Kirk got three potatoes out of the fridge, washed them, rubbed them with salt and put them in the microwave.

Twenty minutes later, they sat down at the kitchen table. Each plate held a petite medium rare flank steak and baked potato topped with butter and sour cream. The plate middle of the table held the baking powder drop biscuits Carla had whipped together.

Daniel uncorked a bottle of wine, filled each glass a third, and passed one to Kirk and Carla. He held up his glass. "A toast. To us. To a new beginning. An ongoing extension of us."

Kirk raised his glass. "Here's to our foundation. To our commitment to us."

Carla lifted her glass. "To what and who we are. To us past, present and future. Together and reunited."

They touched their glasses together, sipped the wine, and set the glasses down.

Daniel cut into his steak and sniffed. "Kirk, good choice".

"Thanks." Kirk cut his steak into bite-size pieces and split his baked potato in quarters. "I'd like to pick up where our conversation left off this morning."

Carla wiped her mouth. "Daniel, are you ready to share more of your story?"

Daniel laid his utensils down, sipped his wine, and spoke. "Ready? Not sure."

Kirk motioned with his knife as he spoke in between bites. "Share what you're comfortable sharing."

Carla laid her hand on Daniel's arm. "Tell what you're ready to tell. If it's nothing. That's all right."

Daniel ate more of his steak and wiped his mouth. "Being a male witch isn't glamorous. Especially when your parents and the witches' council think we're special and need protection."

"Does this have to do with nomenclature?" Carla put her utensils on her empty plate.

"Nomenclature?" Kirk stopped eating and glanced at Daniel and Carla. "Someone cramming for a spelling bee?'

"Nomenclature is cataloging. Stuffing you in a box and labeling you. Like my NMW designation." Carla finished her wine. "Daniel, I'm sorry you went through that."

"Thanks. The pain in the ass was the hovering, constantly peaking over my shoulder wanting to know what I was doing, where I was going."

"No damn privacy." Kirk tossed his napkin on his plate. "They didn't label you NMW, did they?"

CHAPTER SEVENTEEN

"No. My magical traits weren't measurable to quote a few elite wizards and mages." Daniel finished his wine. "I downplayed my magic. Hid what I could do and got through school on general studies."

"Why?" Carla held up the wine bottle. "Refills?"

"No thanks." Kirk held up his glass, swirling the contents. "Plenty left."

Daniel put his hand over his glass. "No more."

Carla corked the bottle and put it in the fridge. "What are your magic traits?"

Daniel cleared his throat. "Extrasensory perception. Second sight and strong cognitive recall. Not picture perfect."

"You got bullied for being good at what you do." Carla placed their dishes in the sink.

" Didn't fit their cookie-cutter ideal." Kirk walked to the counter.

"You hide your gifts. You doubt yourself. You doubt your gifts." Daniel slumped in his chair. "I thought my second sight directed me to Lisa and Rachel. I blew that."

Kirk leaned against the counter. "Nothing is a hundred percent. Nothing is perfect."

Carla looped her arms around Daniel's neck and hugged him. "Did you make any right choices?"

"Yes. Got the condoms. Didn't think I'd use them. Gut and heart said do it." Daniel turned in his chair.

Kirk squirted dish detergent in the sink and filled it with hot water. "You sought me out. Renewed our friendship. Told me you had a strong hunch about that."

"Maybe I'm just rusty. Need to work on using the traits." Daniel stood. "Carla, are you sure you want to sleep with me tonight?"

Carla stood toe-to-toe with Daniel, looking him in the eye, she tapped him close to his heart with her finger. "Yes, I do. Don't doubt your heart."

"I'm washing." Kirk started washing dishes and rinsed them. He held up one of the dripping wet dishes. "Who's drying?"

"I am." Carla grabbed the dish towel, took the dish from Kirk and stacked the dishes as she dried them.

Kirk handed Carla the last dish. "Is one of the other bedrooms inhabitable?"

Carla laughed. "Okay, we're going for the collegiate dictionary words tonight."

Daniel pointed to the laundry room. "Clean sheets on top of the dryer. Room next to the hall bath right up your alley. Plush twin mattress and pillows."

Kirk trotted into the laundry room, chattering as he went. "Ooh, warm, clean sheets. Blankets in there, too, I hope."

Daniel called out as he entered the living room. "Blankets coming. Carla, will you help Kirk and I make the bed?"

Carla grinned, walked over to the laundry room door, leaned in and tweaked Kirk's ass. "Reminder of this afternoon. Will help lull you to sleep."

Kirk walked past her, whistling. He got to the edge of the living room and turned. "I best get a few washcloths too. I might need some relief remembering this afternoon."

Carla shook her head and followed Kirk and Daniel into the guest room.

Ten minutes of pillow fighting, speculating about how the sheets went on the bed, and teasing Kirk about tucking him banter ensued.

"Time to continue our conversation a bit more." Daniel entered his bedroom. Kirk and Carla followed him.

Daniel sat on the bed next to Carla. His hands resting on his knees. "You probably sense my uneasiness."

"I'm not strongly empathetic. Your hesitation and body language yell uncertainty." Carla leaned against him. "Can you tell me why?"

"Like I said earlier, male witches get a dominant magic. Some get two." Daniel leaned back on his hands. "My dominant magic is ESP. I got that *plus*—"

Daniel stopped speaking. He glanced at Carla. She watched him intently. It'd been quite a while since anyone other than Kirk and occasionally his great-grandfather focused with a keen interest on what he was saying.

"This is important for you to mention it again." Carla rested her hand on his thigh. "Go on."

"Please, bro, go ahead," Kirk urged. "We're here for you."

"My other magic is intellect. Details, putting two and two together. Bullies dubbed me super brain." Daniel sighed. "Problem was and is my second sight, and intellect hasn't paired up so great since I sorta turned one of them off. Plus hitting adulthood."

"How so?" Carla sat cross-legged on the bed. "You missed on minor details the times I've seen you use these two together."

"Matters of the heart. I got the hunches with both of my short lived relationships. My heart and gut shouted yes, this is the one. I thought I knew them well." Daniel scrubbed his face with his hands. "Both times I fucked up pretty good."

Carla slipped her arms around Daniel as best she could. She hugged him twice and let go. Taking hold of his hands, she clasped them between hers. "Something Aunt Moriah said when I opened my first business makes a lot of sense. Failing isn't bad. It's first attempt in learning. Her second piece of advice was to a cousin matchmaker. We can only know our own heart."

"I thought I knew mine." Daniel slipped his hands away from hers.

Kirk lay sideways on the bed, facing Daniel and her.

"Did you have any doubts?" Carla laid back on the bed. "Any twinges that said look closer or wait?"

"Doubt a few. I thought I was overthinking things." Daniel stretched out beside her. "With you, the doubts and twinges stopped the longer we were together."

"You, Kirk, and I dared to reveal our true inner selves to each other. We were naked and vulnerable in a way most people aren't." Carla rolled on her side toward Daniel. " We are and were friends, confidantes, and family of choice. We're skeptical on things due to past pain and hurt. We know ourselves and each other well enough to trust being vulnerable with each other again."

Daniel moved closer to her. He laid his hand between her breasts, on her heart. "I feel your heartbeat. I sense the warmth and energy you ooze toward me. You want me."

"Yes, I do. Not sex for sex's sake." Carla inhaled, slowly exhaled and nodded. She was ready to say the word. "Daniel McFarmer, I love you. Probably have for a long time."

"What about Kirk?" Daniel cupped her cheek.

"I love him too." Carla turned her head and kissed Daniel's palm.

Kirk rolled closer to them. "I've got a confession to make."

Daniel looked up at Kirk."I think we're all confessing something."

Kirk put his hand next to Daniel's, between Carla's breasts, close to her heart. "Carla, I fell in love with you again this afternoon."

Carla blew Kirk a kiss. "Thank you both."

"I'm off to bed." Kirk lifted his hand, scooted to the edge of the bed and stood. "Daniel, take good care of our lady. Good night and good lovin'."

"Kirk, wait a moment." Daniel got up and closed the space between Kirk and him. He held his arm out. "Hugs good night, are always welcome."

Kirk and Daniel enveloped each other in a tight embrace and moved apart.

"Daniel, I love you, my best friend and brother of choice." Kirk clasped Daniel's arm.

"I love you too, Kirk. Thanks for being my best friend and chosen brother." Daniel clasped Kirk's arm and let go.

"Good night, Carla. I know you're in good hands." Kirk blew Carla a kiss and exited, closing the bedroom door behind him.

"Carla, I'm listening to my heart." Daniel walked back to the bed, holding out his hand. "I love you. Have for a long time."

"I'm glad you do." Carla took Daniel's hand, stood, and embraced him. She walked to the chair and tossed her clothes on it as she shucked them. "Quick soap and rinse. Then in bed?"

Daniel pulled his shirt over his head, tossed it at the chair and undid his jeans. He shoved his jeans and briefs down over his hips, past his knees and kicked them away from him. He didn't try to hide his arousal. He had an erection that spoke what his heart, mind and psyche were warmly whispering. *You finally found her. Go on love her, and pleasure you both.*

Carla headed toward the bathroom with Daniel right beside her. Warm water, soap and kisses, plus caresses, warmed them further. Rinsing took a bit longer.

Daniel ran his hands up and over Carla, lingering in all the right places. Tweaking her nipples, nipping her neck and thumbing her clitoris until she grasped his arm, ready to orgasm.

"Here or in bed?" Carla released Daniel's arm as he unhurriedly slid his fingers across her clitoris and rested them on her labia.

"Certainly not in here." Daniel shut the shower off. "Waterlogged enough."

Carla exited the shower, handed Daniel his towel and dried off with hers. "Time to cuddle and see what's next."

Daniel hung his towel next to hers. "Time and shared desire. I like the sound of that."

"Intimacy feeds off each other's pleasure." Carla got in the bed, moved to the middle, and rolled onto her side. "I want to taste you."

Daniel put two condom packets on the nightstand. He stashed the box in the nightstand drawer. "I want to taste you too."

Daniel stretched out next to Carla. His feet at her head and his head close to her mons. He softly traced the curve of Carla's hip and thigh with his fingernails, eliciting shivers and moans with each touch. Carla reached between his legs, palming his balls lightly. Her other hand encircled him close to his balls.

"You're beautiful down here. A lot of men don't appreciate a woman's anatomy. They go for parts, and that's it." Daniel parted Carla's labia lips and blew on her clitoris.

Carla jerked closer to Daniel. She puckered her lips, scooted closer, and drew him into her mouth. Groans and shudders erupted. Daniel thrust into her mouth as she started laving his glans and stroking the curve of his ass cheeks. She bobbed her head lower, tightening her lips as she took him deeper into her mouth.

"Aah," Daniel moaned. "Not gonna last if you keep that up."

Carla slowly laved, and suckled her way back up Daniel's cock until she reached his glans, Two quick flicks of her tongue, and she let go. "Delicious. Beautiful how each man tastes different. You're sweet and salty together."

"My turn to taste you." Daniel parted her labia lips. He slipped his arm around her hip and pulled her tighter to him. Watching Daniel dip his head toward her ignited goosebumps and flashes of one of her fantasies. Daniel and she sixty-nining. A balancing act she learned firsthand that didn't always get the anticipated results.

Daniel dragged his tongue lazily across Carla's clitoris. He hesitated, waiting for multiple reactions. Carla pressed tighter to him, rubbing against his face.

"*More, please.*" Carla hunched against him rapidly.

Daniel flicked his tongue quickly around the edge of Carla's clitoris. Over and around with quick short licks. Followed by a slow, languid lave along the swollen nub as he suckled her between his lips. His fingers slid lower, slicking with Carla's increasing wetness. He coated two fingers, easing them inside her, and back out. Twice more, he worked them in and out, increasing his suction on her clit as he rapidly licked her.

Carla stiffened, letting out a low moan. "*I'm there.*"

Wetness coated his tongue and lips. Daniel carefully removed his fingers from Carla. He rolled partially away from her. "*Wow*. Are you okay?"

Carla rolled on her back. Her chest rose and fell with each rapid breath she took. She inhaled and exhaled slowly. She turned toward Daniel, holding her hand out. "Think I'm okay."

Daniel clasped her hand. "Are we ready for more?"

Carla let go of Daniel's hand and tried to sit up. "More?"

"What about this?" Daniel stroked his cock. "I want to come inside you. Bring you more pleasure."

Carla unclenched her hand, letting go of the sheets she clutched. "Easy and slow?"

"Sure. On our sides. Spoon fashion." Daniel rose, tore open a condom packet and eased it on.

Carla reached out, clasped him and squeezed. "Never done it that way."

"Roll on your side facing me after I lay down." Daniel lay on his side. "Scoot toward me, facing me."

Carla scooted closer to him. "Now what?"

"Come closer." Daniel shifted closer to Carla. "Put your leg over my hip. I'll ease into you."

Carla laid her leg over Daniel's hip. Her arm on his waist and snuggled up, pressing themselves against each other.

Daniel reached between them, clasped his condom-covered self firmly and eased into Carla. "Paradise. Wonderous paradise."

"So full. You're inside me. Filling me." Carla tightened as Daniel started stroking her clit again. "How long you going to last?"

Daniel rocked his hips forward, thrusting into Carla deeper. He rocked back, pulling part way out. "Depends on whether you want it very slow. Or faster."

Carla gasped, gripped Daniel's arm and began rocking counter to his thrusts. "Faster. Both of us orgasm together."

"Yes, together." Daniel picked up pace, rocking back and forth quicker.

Carla countered his pace. She tightened, held still, and . . .

Daniel rocked forward, stilled movement and moaned. "*I'm there.*"

"*Me too.*" Carla pressed her lips to his.

Their tongues met, mimicking the thrusts and pulses their bodies vibrated jointly through them. Their breathing slowed as they returned to their bodies from where their volcanic orgasms catapulted them.

Daniel carefully withdrew, keeping a firm grasp on the condom. Carla scooted to the edge of the bed, rose and followed Daniel into the bathroom. Filling the condom with water showed no leaks. No semen smears outside of the condom. Carla tossed the condom in the toilet and flushed. Daniel and she entered the shower, rinsed, and dried. Holding hands, they snuggled close to each other, spooning again as sleep enveloped them.

CHAPTER EIGHTEEN

Carla entered Maxon's banquet room and stopped. Three whirlwind weeks had come and gone faster than either she, Kirk or Daniel expected. Daniel's house was quickly becoming home. A place where the three of them gathered.

"What you think, boss?" Stan asked, walking up to her. "Florist delivered the flowers and centerpiece vases an hour ago."

"I like." Carla tied her apron. "The buffet wall decoration is my favorite. The triplets' names and their ultrasound pictures."

"Ty came up with that. " Stan pointed toward the kitchen entrance. "Rory got his sister Anna involved. She used fabric remnants to make the drapes and tiebacks."

"The colors match the centerpieces." Carla walked to the buffet menu display board. "Are the guests serving themselves?"

"No. Six servers. Three on the buffet line. Three others filling drink orders, busing tables and helping with seating. Rory recruited two of his nephews to help out with clean up." Stan leaned against the drink bar close to the head of the buffet table.

Carla inspected the drink bar. "No alcohol?"

"Ty requested that. A few people may show up with their kids." Stan picked up the clipboard from under the bar and showed it to her.

Carla scanned the menu. Fish, chicken and steak tartare plus red skin potatoes, succotash, and two salads made up the main menu. Assorted breads and rolls would be available on each table. She handed Stan the clipboard. "Stan, you and Rory are awesome. Thanks for overseeing this."

"Glad to help." Stan glanced at his watch. "About ninety minutes until guests start arriving. Anna and Rory are finishing up the baskets people can drop their gift cards in."

"Time enough for me to grab a bite to eat and set up the drink bar." Carla followed Stan into the kitchen.

Hey, boss lady," Chef Rory called out, stepping out from behind a cloud of steam hovering over the stove. "Sandwich, chips, and tall sweet tea on your desk. Enjoy!"

Carla smiled as she entered her office. The tray on her desk held Chef Rory's signature triple-decker BLT cut in half. A bag of her fave salt and vinegar chips and a large glass of sun-brewed sweet tea were next to the sandwich. An envelope and a small wrapped box lay next to the tray. She recognized the handwriting on it. When had Daniel and Kirk dropped it off?

She pulled the envelope and box to her. The envelope read open first. Carla pushed the box away from her. Kirk and Daniel knew she'd open it first and then open the envelope. Attending the class reunion had publicly announced their triad.

She tore open the envelope, took the sheet of paper out, and laid it on the desk. Carla bit into one half of her sandwich as she read the note.

Kirk and Daniel each wrote the first part of the note:

Dearest Carla,

We know you want to open the box. We ask you read this through before you do.

Three weeks ago, we found each other. Reunited and took a chance. A chance that what we had before could ignite again. The chance was worth it.

Daniel wrote the second paragraph:

My heart and psyche told me once, you were the one. I regretted letting you slip away.

Being with you again, my heart and psyche sang out telling me you're the one. I didn't know loving someone could be this beautiful and such a wonderful gift. Thank you for helping me renew my link with my magic traits. I love you, sweetness.

Kirk wrote the third paragraph:

My wolf pinged me the first time we met. Howled and mourned when you disappeared. I didn't know then what my wolf and I know now. You fill the emptiness I've carried for a long time. You were part of my pack then. My heart and wolf joyously sing because you're part of my pack again. I love you, honey.

Daniel and Kirk wrote the last paragraph together:

The box holds our joint birthday gift to you from long ago. Gifting this to you now is part of declaring our intent. What intent you ask? We'll explain this evening. See you at Siobhan's shower.

Love you,

Daniel and Kirk

Carla finished the second half of her sandwich and opened the bag of chips. She fingered the box's bow twice. The soft, velvety feel of the ribbon reminded her of the ribbon she secreted away in her jewelry box until one of her sisters used it as a hair ribbon. Her parents had snatched the ribbon away, tossing it in the trash, stating witches could summon up new ones. Her sisters laughed when she cried over the ragged ribbon. The ribbon Daniel and Kirk hastily wrapped her first birthday present from them with. Two sea shells. She still had the shells. Hiding them in her backpack had saved the shells.

She finished her sandwich and chips, wiped her fingers on a napkin and pulled the box to her. She carefully untied the ribbon. Pocketing it for safekeeping with the other one she managed to covertly fish out of the trash and stash with the shells in her backpack. She opened the box and gasped. Inside was a chain with a ring on it. The ring's stone was her birthstone. The card taped to the inside of the box was partially faded. She could make out part of what it said. *To Carla from your joint boyfriends. Will you go steady with us? Kirk and Daniel*

Carla undid the chain's clasp, put the chain on and fastened the clasp. She closed her fingers around the ring, holding it tight. A knock on her office door sounded. She let go of the ring, wiped her eyes, and gulped the last of her tea. "Come in."

Stan opened the door. "People are starting to arrive."

"Thanks. I'll be out in a moment."

Stan nodded and closed the office door.

Carla pulled a mirror and comb out of her fanny pack. She applied lip gloss, combed her hair and flashed two practice smiles. She dabbed her eyes. Couldn't have people think she was upset. Not many understood happy tears. She put the comb and mirror back in her fanny pack and locked it in her desk drawer. She fingered the ring and chain again. Bridges from the past to the present were solidifying as well as bridge foundations to a future with Daniel and Kirk.

Daniel and Kirk entered the banquet room. Siobhan and Ty stood close to the entrance greeting guests as they entered. Chef Rory's sister, Anna, sat at a table handing out drink tickets and collecting gift cards from the guests. Kirk dropped his, Daniel's, and Carla's three gift cards in the basket. He patted his jacket pocket. Paper rustled inside. Their separate gift for Siobhan and Ty rested inside the envelope in his pocket. A gift certificate for matching quilts for the triplets with their names embroidered on them. Carla's cousin Nick's wife Sandra had put them in touch with the Sylvan Valley quilter.

"Kirk. Daniel." Ty shook hands with them. "Great to see you. Glad you made it."

"Wouldn't miss it." Kirk pulled the envelope out of his jacket pocket. "This is something special for you from Daniel, me and Carla."

Siobhan took the envelope. "You didn't need to do this."

Daniel kissed Siobhan's cheek and whispered, "Yes, we did. It's a special thank-you gift from Carla, Kirk and me."

Siobhan opened the envelope and took the certificate out. "Oh my. Ty, look at this."

Ty faced Daniel and Kirk, embraced them, and stepped back. "Love it. Thank you very much."

"You're welcome." Daniel and Kirk moved further into the banquet room. They sat at a small table middle of the room along one wall close to the drink station.

Carla set two glasses of ginger beer on the table. "Did you give Ty and Siobhan the gift certificate?"

"Yes," Kirk answered, sipping his ginger beer. "They loved it."

"Glad they did." Carla leaned against the wall. "Stan will bring your plates in a moment. He and Chef Rory set aside a bit of everything for you."

"Looks like everyone turned out." Daniel sampled his ginger beer and set the glass down. "Do you know everyone?"

"A few." Carla pulled an empty chair over to the table and sat down. "Older couple sitting with Ty and Siobhan is her Aunt Elana and James. Next table over is Siobhan's sisters Gladys, Teresa and Nance, and their spouses."

Kirk coughed and nudged Daniel. "Don't be obvious. I think Aunt Naomi and Aunt Zelda are about to swoop down on us."

Daniel groaned. "Sure does. Can't put it off."

Aunt Zelda pulled two chairs to the table. She sat in one. Aunt Naomi in the other. They folded their arms across their chests and stared at Daniel and Kirk.

"I've got customers." Carla hastily rose and moved away from the table.

"Aunt Zelda," Kirk began, glancing around her. "Why are you angry?"

"Yeah, Aunt Naomi," Daniel said. "Same question."

Aunt Zelda lowered her arms. "When were you supposed to check in?"

Aunt Naomi nodded at Aunt Zelda. "What she said."

"By the full moon." Daniel leaned forward. "That's another three weeks off."

"Your formal match form said no texts, calls or emails for seventy-two hours. It's way past that." Aunt Naomi pointed at Kirk. "You forget to charge your phone again?"

Kirk held up both hands. "No. Didn't have time to return calls or report in other than to Carla and Daniel."

"You've been with her the entire time?" Aunt Zelda asked.

Daniel pointed at Aunt Zelda and Aunt Naomi. "Our meal approaches. Thanks for checking in. The three of us are fine."

Kirk kissed his Aunt Zelda's cheek. "When there's more to tell, we'll let you know."

Daniel pulled both chairs out of the way. He hugged his Aunt Naomi. "Thank you for caring. We've got this."

Both women walked away, glancing back twice and shaking their heads. Kirk dropped into his chair. "I love that they care. I wish they didn't see us as teens needing herding."

Daniel waited for Stan to place their plates. "Thanks Stan."

"You bet." Stan started to turn, hesitated and turned back. "If it's any consolation, they do that with Rory and me, too."

Daniel nodded. "Matchmaker and surrogate parents."

"Yup. Enjoy your meals." Stan made his way back into the kitchen.

Carla came back to the table, holding a plate of salad. "Safe to join you?"

"For the moment." Daniel spread his napkin on his lap. "Telling your Aunt and matchmaker mind their own business ain't easy."

"You got that right!" Kirk picked up his utensils as he added, "Especially when your business and theirs are the same thing!"

Carla pressed her lips tight against each other. She looked around the room. People were busy talking and eating or socializing. Maybe no one heard them. Well, except Stan, who walked by her and winked, grinning like a Cheshire cat. She sat next to Daniel and began eating.

Conversations and people milling about continued. Chef Rory and Stan cleared the buffet table and set up the dessert area. A large sheet cake sat center of the table. On one side were mugs, dessert plates, napkins and utensils. Coffee urns, hot water, tea bags, mugs, plus sweetener and cream on the opposite side. Another hour passed as people helped themselves to dessert and continued mingling.

Ty and Siobhan walked to the center of the room. Ty rapped on the drink bar. Conversations stopped. People sat down.

"Thank you all for coming." Ty clasped Siobhan's hand. "You're generosity is amazing. Sylvan Valley's Women and Children Foodbank plus Cauldron Falls' Foodbank pantries are restocked."

Applause sounded. Siobhan held up her hand. "Thank you to everyone for your gifts and kindness. Thank you, Carla, for hosting our event here at Maxon's."

Ty held up his and Siobhan's hands. "Siobhan accepted my full moon proposal."

Cheers rang out. Ty waited for the noise to die down. "I understand our newest co-alphas, Daniel and Kirk, would like to say a few words."

Daniel glanced at Kirk. Kirk nodded. They rose and walked to the center of the room.

"I'll go first." Daniel turned around as he continued speaking. "Community takes all of us. I'm amazed and proud to see many of Cauldron Falls and Sylvan Valley residents here. Thank you for embracing diversity and change. You're awesome."

A few hoots and cheers sounded and quieted as Kirk moved up beside Daniel.

"Co-alphaing is new. Different and comes with challenges. Tasks that a lot of us face daily. We're stronger together than individually. We each bring value and experience to the table. Let's continue working together to make Cauldron Falls and Sylvan Valley stronger and forward moving."

More applause and cheers broke out.

Daniel and Kirk thrust their arms in the air and waved their hands. The cheers and applause dwindled.

Daniel and Kirk spoke at the same time. "Carla, would you join us, please?"

Carla pointed to herself.

Daniel and Kirk continued speaking together. "Yes, you."

Ty set a chair between Daniel and Kirk. Daniel and Kirk patted the seat.

Carla moved forward and sat on the chair.

Daniel took hold of her left hand. Kirk held her right hand. Each went down on one knee. Stuck their free hand into their pants pocket and each pulled out a box.

Daniel let go of her hand first. "These last few weeks are some of the happiest times for me. Being with you. Rebuilding our connection and finding out who we are now."

Kirk let go of her other hand. "Building a future together is important. Understanding where you come from and the foundation of us helps us do this."

"Carla," Daniel and Kirk spoke in unison as they each opened the boxes they held. "Will you marry us? Be our mate and full moon match forever and always?"

"Yes, Daniel and Kirk, I will be your mate and accept your proposal." Carla stood, holding out her hands. "Will you marry me and be my full moon forever and always mates?"

Daniel and Kirk yelled together, "Yes. Yes. Full moon mates now and always."

EPILOGUE

Carla looked around Maxon's outside garden. Floral canopies marked each of the four corners of the square. One corner for each of them and the fourth for their exit as a confirmed mated triad. The full moon overhead illuminated the center of the circle where she, Kirk and Daniel would pledge their future together.

Six months ago, Daniel, Kirk and her had embarked on a discovery journey. A journey that left them questioning their past, reviewing where each of them had been and where each of them emerged ready, strong and secure in themselves. Moving past their fears and hesitations, embracing who they are here and now took a bit of doing.

Painting Daniel's home, now their joint home, had turned into a six-week fest. A fest that had them talking about what they'd dreamed about as kids, what they needed as they matured, and what each of them wanted and needed now and in the future. Kirk had drawn up plans for expanding the house so that each had a bedroom suite of their own. The guest room cottage would happen in the spring. For now, their triad was their focus.

Music sounded. Daniel entered from the corner on the back right. His decorated canopy contained stars and half-moon-shaped lights entwined with his favorite flower, midnight blue Delphinums. The moon and stars signified his acceptance of his second sight and the Delphinums his understanding of his gift. His personal insight spoken from his heart and psyche. He wore a blue robe the hue of midnight. A gift from his Aunt Naomi.

Strains of the next song began. Kirk entered from the left back corner canopy wearing a brown earth-tone robe. His canopy decorations symbolized his love of the earth. Daisies, lilacs and wildflowers with orange, green and yellow twinkling lights adorned the canopy. Intermixed with the flowers and lights were miniature stuffed wolves. A gift from his Aunt Zelda.

Music changed again. Her song began. Carla picked up her bouquet and stepped under her decorated canopy. Multicolored tulips intertwined with baby's breath and myrtle sprigs adorned the canopy interspersed with multicolored hearts. Her bouquet matched the canopy's floral arrangement. Her multi-hued lavender gown, tailor-made for her by Siobhan's wedding dressmaker, matched the aura outline she saw every time she looked at Daniel and Kirk.

Center of the circle stood Sylvan Valley's Justice of the Peace Ralph O'Shay and his wife Tracey, high priestess of the Witches Council and officiant of weddings. Kirk stood on one arc of the circle. Daniel another. Carla handed her bouquet to Tracey, nodded, and joined hands with Daniel and Kirk.

Ralph spoke first. "Vows are a personal choice. The state doesn't require anything more than those seeking legal documentation of their joining to freely declare their intent. Do you, Daniel, Kirk and Carla, freely declare your intent to legally join as mates?"

Kirk, Daniel and Carla responded together, "We do."

Tracey spoke next. "Lupa, the One and personal deities bring together those that seek love with open accepting hearts. Love that began many years ago has found its way back home again, uniting the three of you. By the power of the One, Luna and your personal deities, I witness your matches. I witness your mate choices. Do you, Carla, Daniel and Kirk acknowledge your match choice? Do you each freely choose those present as a mate of your own?"

Carla answered first. "I freely choose Daniel and Kirk as my mate choices. I swear this by Luna, the One and my personal deities."

Kirk replied next. "I freely choose Carla and Daniel as my mate choices. I swear this by Luna, the One and my personal deities."

Daniel responded last. "I freely choose Carla and Kirk as my mate choices. I swear this by Luna, the One and my personal deities."

Tracey and Ralph place their hands on Kirk's, Daniel's and Carla's. Tracey and Ralph spoke in unison. "By the powers of the state, the Witches Council and the Matchmakers Guild, your match choices are recorded, sanctified and blessed. May Luna, the One and your personal deities bless you now and always. Love strongly and well."

Carla, Kirk and Daniel stepped into the circle, their arms around each other. They'd each found a mate of their own worth keeping and loving again and again.

Don't miss out!

Visit the website below and you can sign up to receive emails whenever Solara Gordon publishes a new book. There's no charge and no obligation.

https://books2read.com/r/B-A-RAUJ-QLLCE

BOOKS 2 READ

Connecting independent readers to independent writers.

Did you love *A Mate of Their Own*? Then you should read *Three Hearts Entwined*[1] by Solara Gordon!

What do you do when two law enforcement officers take more than a passing interest in you?

That's what Cassandra Sullivan wants to know.

Cassandra overhears Cauldron Falls Sheriff Dakota Knox and Sylvan Valley Deputy Police Chief

Logan Jones refer to her as 'our lady'. This marks a change in their three-way friendship.

Up to now, things haven't involved candid conversations and romantic assertions.

With Dakota and Logan pursuing her, Cassandra is at odds with who to choose. Will she choose one. . or both?

Read more at https://solaragordon.com/.

---

1. https://books2read.com/u/3y28qe

2. https://books2read.com/u/3y28qe

Also by Solara Gordon

Cascade Bay
Love Reborn
Reunited By Choice
Love's Triple Play
Three Hearts In Love
For the Love of Three

Cauldron Falls
Believe In Love
Home for the Holidays
Three Hearts Entwined
A Mate of Their Own
A Christmas Reunion

Peyton Corners
Falling for You
Caught by Love's Slow Burn

Standalone
A Heart's Desire
To Love You Again

To Love You Again

Watch for more at https://solaragordon.com/.

About the Author

Solara loves and lives with her partner of 21 years in the Metro DC area. What started out as a bi-coastal romance soon settled on one coast.

A vivid imagination keeps her busy creating her next fascinating romance. She enjoys creating unique characters and watching their journeys unfold. "Love freely given multiplies and will return endlessly" is a key aspect of her stories. Add in alternative lifestyles and her love for the paranormal, and the uncommon becomes the norm in many of her stories.

Her day job in the financial services industry pays the bills while she pens her erotic tales.

Read more at https://solaragordon.com/.